24/04/22

Please return/renew this item by the last
date shown. Books may also be renewed
by phone or internet.

💻   www3.rbwm.gov.uk/libraries

☎   01628 796969 (library hours)

☎   0303 123 0035 (24 hours)

www.rbwm.gov.uk

Royal Borough
of Windsor &
Maidenhead

ELLY

ELLY

Maike Wetzel

translated by Lyn Marven

SCRIBE

Melbourne • London

Scribe Publications
2 John St, Clerkenwell, London, WC1N 2ES, United Kingdom
18–20 Edward St, Brunswick, Victoria 3056, Australia
3754 Pleasant Ave, Suite 100, Minneapolis, Minnesota 55409 USA

First published in English by Scribe in 2020
Originally published in German in 2018 by Schöffling & Co.
Verlagsbuchhandlung GmbH

The translation of this work was supported
by a grant from the Goethe-Institut.    GOETHE INSTITUT

Typeset in Garamond Premier by the publishers
Printed and bound in the UK by CPI Group (UK) Ltd,
Croydon CR0 4YY

Scribe Publications is committed to the sustainable use of
natural resources and the use of paper products made responsibly
from those resources.

9781912854127 (UK edition)
9781950354191 (US edition)
9781925849165 (Australian edition)
9781925938197 (ebook)

Catalogue records for this book are available from the
National Library of Australia and the British Library.

scribepublications.co.uk
scribepublications.com
scribepublications.com.au

This story is not my story. I'm not sure which one of us it belongs to. It's lying there in the street, it's sleeping in our house, and yet it's always one step ahead of me. I want to write it down to exorcise it, so I can catch my breath again. I've been running for so long. I'm tired and weary. The boy next door is sitting in my lap. Yesterday he bit his lip open. The blister has filled with pus.

I remember a time when I'm awake and alive. I see myself. A bounding, freckled child. I run as fast as I can. The soles of my feet pound the asphalt. My heart is beating in my mouth. I run so I can feel how strong I am. My legs stick out of my short blue shorts. I am proud of the fact that a boy wore them before me. I feel brave in these shorts. The summer air caresses my legs. The gravel on the tarmac digs into my soles. My feet lift off from the ground. I am floating a hand's breadth above the asphalt. I glide round the corner, down the small alleyway, to the stream. The water is brown and peaty, the riverbed is sand. I can see fish through the gaps between the planks on the wooden bridge. Dark streaks against a white background. I fly all the way to the woods. I spread my arms and swim through the air. I am happier than I'm allowed to be. I float over everything; over people, over the television in our living room. Then I plunge downwards. I'm falling. My scream wakes me.

Come back soon, we need to investigate, the doctors say. But there's nothing to investigate. My body is strong. It's something else that is oppressing me, choking me, almost stopping me from breathing.

I hold on to the story because nobody tells it. Silence is part of the family. It's hard to describe — I can't put my finger on it — because silence doesn't consist of saying nothing. My parents and I talk about this and that, but the truth falls through the cracks, down deep. No sentence catches it. They say death is an end to life, but there is a life beyond death. People live on in the stories we tell each other. Even things we don't talk about live on; they come back again in a different form.

This story is also a play. Appearing are: my parents, Judith and Hamid. My little sister, Elly, sits breathing down our tiny father's neck. My mother holds me by the hand. The stage is lit by sunshine. Then Elly disappears.

She exits into the dark backdrop. A gravestone thunders down onto the stage. We cry, we wail, we tear our hair out. Each one of us tumbles on our own, alone, into the blackness at the back of the stage. Finally Elly appears, transformed. She is much older, her eyes are dark. We stare at her. Then my mother puts her arms around her and embraces her. We surround the girl, cover her with our bodies. We are vampires. We shroud her. All that remains is a bare skeleton. A small child enters. It laughs and picks up a broom. It sweeps the stage clean. Then it throws the broom into the audience, crosses its legs and sits down, and says: So far, so good.

QUEEN

In the beginning is the pain. Sharp and spiky, it bores into my guts. It takes my breath away. I double over, whimper, groan. Then it's over. The pain is gone. Suddenly I am free. I sit up again. I breathe in. I try to go back to sleep. But the cramps come back. The pain hollows me out. My moaning wakes my mother. She looks at me blearily. I'm lying on the sofa, in the dark. When the cramps come, I forget myself. You're becoming a woman, my mother says. I can't catch a breath now. The pain constricts my throat. My mother tries to hold me and rock me, but her hands are too clumsy. As if she were wearing boxing gloves. Help, I want to cry, please help me. What my mother would prefer to do is make her excuses and step away from this imposition, or keel over herself. Instead she frantically tips tablets onto the table, fumbles for her phone, asks for advice.

The woman on the other end thinks we should come in. My mother says to me: Darling everything will be fine. Her boyfriend will drive us to the hospital. I give a loud groan. My mother quickly changes tack. She fetches the hot water bottle, makes tea. I feel the pain tugging at the skin on my face. My mother doesn't wait for her boyfriend. She calls a taxi. The hospital admits us.

Appendix, the doctor in the emergency ward says, couldn't be more obvious. My mother says: But my daughter had it out two years ago. The doctor scribbles on his notepad. He's not receiving on this frequency. My mother chirps again: Can't you see the scar? But the doctor's pupils are reflected on the screen of his smartphone. My gaze roams around the room, looking for something to hang on to. An elephant on a poster. My eyes trace its folds, its tusks. The pain is sneaking up. From behind, like thunder behind clouds. My belly goes rigid, it is threatening to burst. A worm pushes its way through my guts. It threatens to blow me up. I can't think any more, I can only feel. That's what it will be like when you're older and have children, the doctor in the emergency ward says. I'm only a child myself. At least in the eyes of the law. I haven't played with dolls for a long time. The only thing I speak to my mother about is empty yoghurt pots and heaps of clothes. I whinge at her. Since she found this business informatics guy on the internet, she has lost her mind. I call him Hugo, although his name is Adam. He smiles and ignores it. I have stopped hoping he will leave my mother. There's nothing I hope for any more. If anything, I hope that I'll grow breasts finally. That would be a step in the right direction. Those mounds give you power. I'm flat and angry. Sometimes I imagine waking up in the morning, transformed into a beetle. Ideas like that make me laugh. That makes time pass faster. I'm tired all the time. Only the pain wakes me. It returns with a vengeance. It rams into my belly.

The doctor hooks me up to the drip and puts me on the list for an operation. He wants to remove my appendix. My mother says again: Your colleague already took it out. The doctor prods my rigid belly. My mother stops fighting. She gives my name, our health insurance details. She called me Almut because of the north. Because of the stiff breeze on the island of Sylt, where she has never been; because of the tall blond boy that she never kissed, because she doesn't like tall blonds; because of the seagulls, whose cries make her melancholy; and because of the seaweed and the salt which no longer cling to her legs: now it's dark stretchy jeans with all their poisonous dyes instead. I'm also called Almut because it contains the German for courage, *Mut*, and my mother believed the name would give me some. I'm meant to grow big and strong. My mother looks at me and sees herself lying in the hospital bed. She strokes my hair. I shrink away from her hand. The doctor puts the cannula in my arm. The coldness of the anaesthetic runs into me. The lights over me glare. The anaesthetist counts backwards. Ten, nine, eight. I don't even hear seven.

I'm still woozy from the anaesthetic when I see Ines for the first time. After that, nothing is ever the same again. My mouth is full of cotton wool, my eyelids are heavy. I'm a stone coming to life. Ines has the bed by the window. The backlight conjures a halo for her. Her features remain in shadow. On her bedside table on wheels are bottles with astronaut food inside them. Ines tells me that the yellow liquid tastes like banana, the red like strawberries. I'm envious. She eats as if she has already flown to the moon. I get boring invalid food. Only a tiny scar graces my belly. The loop in my bowel was untwisted just in time. Ines on the other hand went the whole hog: she got her appendix to burst. The poison flooded through her body. She seems to be an arm's length ahead of me in everything. I'm thirteen, she is fourteen. *Iiii-nes*. The syllables suit her. First the expression of disgust, the devastating judgement. Then the sweet-talking ending, the salvation. Ines is neither particularly pretty nor ugly. Nothing about her is remarkable. Her brown hair is smooth, parted in the middle; her nightie is white like the sheets, starched. I dream about her. Water, waves, misadventure. Ines saves me from all of them. She pulls me out of the maelstrom by my hair. When I wake up, I tell her about it. Ines wrinkles her forehead. For the first time she encourages me to carry on talking. I tell her everything. My voice trembles. Ines says nothing. I feel naked. Ines is so certain, so strong. She doesn't need words to make me understand. I can sense her superiority. She makes the roots of my hair stand up. She is a queen. I recognise that immediately. I don't need anyone to tell me. I know a queen when I see one. A queen has nothing to lose. That's why she gets everything. Suddenly I'm wide awake.

I'm happy to be in hospital, because I'm with Ines. Ines on the other hand misses her school. She paints me a picture of a place full of colour, light, music. The pupils there dance, paint, sing. They make pottery, build dens, bake bread, survey the land. Not every child is allowed to go to this school. Even Ines had to take a test. The headmistress gave her watercolours and a dampened sheet of paper. Ines dabbed the paintbrush over it. The colours ran into one another, mixed together. Ines gave her picture to the headmistress, who studied the colours. She scrutinised Ines, compared her with her painting. Those messy daubs were Ines's ticket to paradise. This is how I imagine the school. The walls and roofs are steeply angled like the sides of a diamond. The garden is wild. Overgrown. Meadows, wildflowers, a field of wheat. A pond with waterlilies. A frog croaks.

The midges dance above the reeds. A hedge shields the garden from the street. Sentries stand at the entrance gate. The two teachers shake every student's hand. They check their body temperature and their eyes. Anyone who seems too cold has to run a lap of the building. Ines is always the right temperature. The nurses in the hospital are bewildered when they remove the thermometer from Ines's body. They don't know that Ines secretly chills it while the sisters rub me down with a washcloth. Ines doesn't want to go home. She just wants to have everything under control. She wants to be the one who decides how she is doing. Despite her successful deception with the thermometer, Ines will have to stay in the clinic for a long time yet. But I'm meant to be leaving. After the weekend you'll be back home, the nurses say. Aren't you happy? I look at Ines. She is looking out of the window.

The walls in the hospital are coated with dirt-repellent paint. A colour like eggshells. Snot and tears roll off these walls. When no one is looking, I test it out. My mother brings me apples, a book. I ignore her. Since she left my father, I have been punishing her. I only ask my mother for one thing: I want to go to Ines's school. My mother refuses. Laughing, she says she's not one of those types. She doesn't dream in pastels and she doesn't believe in reincarnation. Anger wells up in me. I blow my mother out. Make her fade away. After a quarter of an hour of silence, she gives up. She says goodbye. Only her apples are left behind. One of them is gleaming red. It has a bruise. I weigh it in my hand. The apple smells juicy. I give it to Ines. She pierces it with a rusty needle. I fold my hands, bow my head. Ines anoints me with its juice. She says it heals all wounds. She says I'm something special, like a precious stone. That I just need to be polished. That what makes me special is encrusted, it only catches the light for a moment at a time. But that I'm in luck: Ines recognises me despite everything. She promises to help me. I don't need my mother's permission to go to her school, she says. I'm the only one that matters. She says I could pass the test. She prepares me. We train hard.

I need to learn everything from scratch again. Standing, walking, even the way I sit is wrong. Ines practises with me. I have to repeat everything a thousand times. At night she wakes me and asks me what music I like, how old I am, or what my favourite colour is. Quickly, I say: Waltzes, eleven and red. Ines tucks me up again and kisses me on the forehead. I don't forget how old I actually am or that I much prefer green. But I'm a good pupil. I'm a quick learner. I know what my teacher wants to hear. Ines is pleased with my progress. I'm pleased that she is pleased. She changes my preferences, my hobbies, my experiences. I accept everything willingly. Ines says my name doesn't suit me. My real name, my secret name, is Eleonore. She calls me Elly. I answer to it. Ines transforms me. She gives me new clothes and even a wig. I get changed in the bathroom. When I open the door, Ines stares at me. Shocked, I ask: Have I got everything right? I pluck at my hair

hesitantly. Ines doesn't say anything. Stiff as a mario-
nette, she reaches a hand out to me. She pulls me onto
her knees. I'm too big for that, but it doesn't bother
her. She holds me in her arms, rocks me, and hums. I
keep completely still. The wig is black and woolly. My
own hair is blonde and thin. Ines doesn't care that the
wig looks fake. She strokes my pretend hair. A cleaner
catches us. She laughs at the sight. I feel helpless, angry.
Ines is shaking. She is in danger of losing her composure, I can see it. But she pulls herself together. The next
minute she is my queen again. Powerful, untouchable.
The cleaner says we should go outside, get some fresh
air, not just lock ourselves away in the room. We fling
ourselves onto our beds. She swishes the mop around
us. We let her talk. The grown-ups believe it's all just a
game.

The doctor calls the children from the room next
door to my bedside. They are allowed to watch. The
plastic thread on my scar is about to be taken out.
The doctor pulls my pyjama trousers down below my
belly button. I'm afraid they will slip further. I try not
to breathe. The doctor plucks at the red bulge on my
skin with tweezers. Finally he catches the blue thread.
A boy is staring at my stomach. He pulls a face, he's
disgusted. I hate him. Ines walks out. Immediately the
room seems darker. The doctor holds the blue thread up

in the air. We'll soon be shot of you, he jokes. He praises me: The wound is healing in textbook fashion. When he has gone, Ines passes me her rusty needle. I dip it in the toilet. Then I pick my scar apart with it. Ines helps me. We spread the sheet over the blood. The cloth soaks it up. The fever comes almost at once. The nurses can't explain it. They give me juice. I spit it out when they aren't looking.

At night, when all the sick children are asleep, Ines dances for me. She loosens the curtain from its hooks, wraps it around her body like a veil. It's dark in the room. The only light is from the moon. The darkness is velvety. It envelops us. A tawny owl calls. A night nurse is patrolling the corridor. She walks past our door at regular intervals. She never comes into the room. I'm convinced Ines stops her. Ines doesn't need to issue orders. She can control thoughts. I believe it. I'm not allowed to talk while Ines is dancing. Even a cough will break the spell. Ines dances without music. Her face is motionless; she gazes off into infinity. She seems to get her instructions from there. Only her body is here with me. Ines's movements are carefully described. She doesn't hop, she doesn't sway. It is a sublime dance, a confident dance. Her arms swing, they reach far into space. Her hands stretch up into the air, almost as high as the stars in the sky. Then her body collapses in on itself. She crouches down for a second, pirouettes, rises up again. Her movements tell me what I can't understand. She is letting me in on a secret. Ines is beautiful when she dances. I want to touch her, but I don't dare.

My pyjamas stick to my body. I am enjoying the fever, my weakness, the inner turmoil. Ines is my ally. We live in a twilight realm. Our sick room belongs to us and us only. It is a capsule. We are floating through space. Ines already has her astronaut food, and I am weightless. I don't know which way is up or down any more, or who I really am. I am merging into Elly. As soon as the other children are asleep, the ward belongs to us. Ines and I haunt the place. We borrow shoes and lipstick from the nurses' room. We play tag under the X-ray machine. Sometimes at night we even steal out onto the lawn. We lie down in the grass. We shiver together. We make ourselves ill. No one is allowed to cure us. We hold hands. Ines says I'm nearly there. That I'll soon understand. That I'll reach enlightenment. As she says it, I can already sense the peace that she is promising me. As soon as we're alone, I turn into Elly, and Ines spoils me. She feeds me forbidden sweets, she teaches me new songs. We chase each other. If I manage to catch Ines, I'm allowed to hug her. I'm happy as Elly.

I feel free. As Elly, I'm allowed to be daft. I can joke with Ines, tease her. As Elly, I have power. I'm close to Ines. I am her creation. It's not about going to her school any more. I just want to be with Ines.

In the hospital we live in the eternal present. Ines and I know that. We use it to our advantage. During the day we doze on our beds. Questions from our parents or from the doctors and orderlies vanish into smoke. They don't touch us. We shrug our shoulders. We don't exchange a word in front of the adults. We don't even look at each other. We both just happen to be lying in the same room, we both just happened to have a twisted intestine. The rest is none of the grown-ups' business. Elly only emerges after the sun goes down. I'm looking forward to it already. Our experiment seems to be working. The adults are at a loss. I'm feverish, my blood is poisoned. I'm allowed to stay with Ines. She tells me stories about death. I try to understand her. Our room smells of spray alcohol. I wrinkle my nose. Ines says: You're making progress. She's right. I walk more consciously. I breathe more deeply. Even my forehead seems to be higher and smoother. Just make a little bit more effort, says Ines. Then you'll be there. At my school, everyone is happy. There are no pressures, no differences. They just have to accept you. She says she will intercede on my behalf. I clasp her hand gratefully. But she withdraws it. I'm only allowed to touch her as Elly. All of a sudden that bothers me. Who is this Elly? Does Ines like her or me? I'm not allowed to ask her any questions, I know that, otherwise she'll drop me without a second thought. But the doubt eats away at me. I can hardly concentrate on my role. I scuff my feet. But the way Elly walks is more like a skip. Are my feet sticking to the floor deliberately? My performance is sloppy. I use the wrong phrases, I forget bits of my costume. Ines reprimands me. I quickly slip back into my role. As Elly, I put her in a gracious mood. Ines forgives my mistakes. She says she just wants the best for me, to look out for me. That's why I have to learn to always do as she says. I swear obedience and silence until death. In the dawning light, Ines kisses me right next to my mouth. She strokes my wig hair again and murmurs: Sleep, my little one, sleep yourself better. I close my eyes.

In front of the hospital is a bus stop. I can see it from the window. A man is perched there with a plastic bag by his side. His face is ashen grey. He has been sitting there for days. No bus comes. I pull the curtain across the window. I'm uneasy, can't eat any more. I have questions; I'm looking for the answers. I wait for an opportunity. Eventually Ines disappears into the bathroom. I rummage through her cupboard. The only thing I find is clean underwear. But just as I close the door, I spot the corner of a photograph. It is sticking out from under the cupboard. Ines is a few years younger in the photo, but I recognise her immediately. The man and woman behind her are her parents. They come to visit now and then. Ines's mother has long, chestnut-brown hair and a nose ring. Her gaze is clear and sharp. Her father is shorter than his wife and smiles benignly, like a pensive troll. The sea splashes behind them. The honeyed light of the setting sun glistens on the waves. It's a holiday snap. I know the scene, the smiles, the show of unity. Our family photos don't look much different. It's not the beach that transfixes me, it's the person next to Ines. This person makes me catch my breath. She is smaller than Ines. Her black hair curls softly. They stick out in all directions, as if they are electrically charged. Even this girl's clothes are familiar. I wear them every night. The sound of the toilet flushing in the bathroom. I quickly shove the photo back under the cupboard.

At night, Ines and I play as if nothing has happened. I am Elly, she is my queen. We make our way down to the hospital's basement. Long, empty corridors link the individual buildings. There are no windows, just bare concrete and pipes. Down there is where the spare beds are parked too. They have empty mattresses and clean sheets. They are waiting for the next patient. The people who lay on these beds last were discharged or died. Ines reckons the nurses store the dead bodies down here too. The freezers must be somewhere, she says. I nod. I wonder whether Ines has ever seen a dead person before. I don't ask. I just need to look at her to know the answer. For the first time, I notice the gleam in her eyes. Her pupils flicker. I want to turn round. I look for the stairs. I want to go back to our room. But Ines throws me onto one of the beds. She pushes me through the corridors. Faster and faster. The walls blur. I don't know where we are any more. I shout: Enough, stop. But Ines doesn't want to. She swings herself up onto the bed, next to me. It still doesn't come to a stop. The bed whizzes through the basement, past a thousand shadows. Ines laughs. The echo bounces off the bare walls. I cling on to the mattress. I try to grab Ines's flying hair and lose my grip. I fall onto the hard concrete. The bed carries on rolling. Ines throws herself on top of me. Her body is much heavier than I expect. I feel myself crumple. My heart stops beating for a moment. Then my pulse races. Ines kneels on my chest, victorious. She says: Now it's your turn. But I don't want to play any more. I pull the wig off my head. Ines's expression turns angry and cold. She disappears into the labyrinth of the basement without me. I clamber to my feet. All alone, I keep wandering down the same corridors over and over. The light goes out. The dark makes me afraid. It's the crack of light under the door which finally shows me the way. I drag myself up the stairs.

I'm staring at a book. After an appropriate length of time, I turn the page. I'm not reading. I can't think any more, either. My thoughts splinter like thin ice with every step I take. Ines is perched on her bed, next to mine, filing her nails. The noise scours the back of my eyes. As long as the sun is shining, everything is like it used to be. Then evening comes. No sooner has the nurse switched on the emergency lighting in the corridor than Ines orders me into the bathroom. That's where Elly's clothes are hidden, in the cistern. I fish the knotted plastic bag out of the water. But this time when I start to get changed, I hesitate. I don't have much time to put my thoughts in order. Ines is waiting outside for me. I venture out without my costume. Ines stares at me. Her voice slices through my eardrum. She orders me back in. I refuse to go. I tell her she is messing me around. I want to know when I can finally take the entrance exam for her school, why is she torturing me? Ines gets angry. She hisses that I don't understand anything, that I'm not worthy. I don't budge. I take some scissors and cut up Elly's jumper. Ines moans. She snatches the bundle of clothes out of my hand. I manage to grab it back. We fight, wrestle, lock jaws. Ines's breath burns my face. I accuse her. I say she isn't interested in me. Why can't I just be myself? Each of us is clinging on to a leg of Elly's trousers. The material cracks and rips. Ines says: You're ruining everything. That's the last thing she says to me. It's over. From this moment on, I'm dead to Ines. She even leaves me the destroyed clothes. I gather up the scraps. I sew them together again in secret. I find a little box with needle and thread in the nurses' room. I lay the mended clothes on the table. But Ines still looks right through me. She doesn't even look up when I throw chocolate on her bed. I'm sad, but I don't cave in. I don't want to be someone else any more.

My mother's hair has white streaks all of a sudden. She worries about me. I tell her she needs to stop that. She wails: Don't you want to get better again? What's holding you back? She suspects that my roommate is behind my transformation. Ines is lying next to us. She plays deaf, but secretly listens in while my mother whispers. I didn't speak to my mother much before, but since I met Ines, she means nothing to me. Less than nothing. I don't need her. To her face, I claim that I don't care about Ines either. I don't talk to her; I don't even look at her. My mother ignores my charade. She wants to split us up. The doctor helps her. While I'm sleeping, the sister releases the brake on my bed. She wheels me to another floor. When I wake up I see a white head of hair next to me. The hair rattles as it breathes. The room smells of old woman. I don't know where I am. Ines is

27

gone. I can't find her. The ward door is locked. Patients aren't allowed out. The doctor says: It's for your own safety. You need to get better. Your mind isn't willing. He is using it against me. I have a lot of time to think.

I'm not listening to the doctor's questions or his advice any more. Even the groans coming from the old woman in the bed next to me get quieter when I think about Ines. I miss her. At night I stand by the window and watch the lawn in front of the hospital. Now, light from a torch is flashing at the spot where Ines and I lay in the grass together. It takes a while before I understand Ines's Morse code. When I work out her message, my heart feels warm and soft. But I can't get out. The ward door is locked. I want to go to Ines. I know she is longing for me too. At this moment I don't care that it's only Elly that Ines wants. I'm so alone that it hurts underneath my breastbone. The old woman next to me babbles; she reaches into thin air, points to me. Obediently, I take my pills. I don't count the pills any more. I swallow them down. I eat and drink and don't pick my scar open any more. The doctor is satisfied. My mother raises her hopes. She dyes her hair. But at night I read Ines's flashes in the dark. They are the only thing that keeps me going.

The crocuses are poking their heads out of the earth in front of the hospital. I can see the brightly coloured dots in among the brown from my window on the third floor. The doctor adds his squiggle to the bottom of my discharge papers. Satisfied, he puts his hands into his white coat. He says something about a miracle, he congratulates me and my mother, gives her the suitcase and me his hand. I secretly cross my fingers behind my back. My mother thanks the doctor; he praises her patience, recommends a holiday. My mother says the flight is already booked. We're off tomorrow. Surprise! She smiles at me. My gaze is rigid. We're catching a plane to an island, she says. We'll do whatever you want. My gaze drifts towards the window. My mother assures me I'll like it. The hotel has four stars. We walk through the hospital corridors. My soles slap against the PVC.

The other patients shuffle along the corridor in their dressing gowns and tracksuit trousers. Some are pulling their drip or an oxygen cylinder behind them. They don't look up. I ask for a piece of cake from the shop, but my mother steers me out of the door. She doesn't want to stay in the hospital any longer than necessary. We need to pack. Panic starts to rise in me.

For the first time in months, I'm lying in my own bed. I walk my feet up the wall. Higher and higher until I can flip over backwards. There's no one there for my well-earned applause. Next door, I can hear my mother's clothes hangers squeaking. She is looking for her linen trousers for the holiday. Once it's dark, I creep out of the house. The door falls into the lock with a click. The street is damp. The tarmac is steaming. Petrol shimmers in rainbow colours on a puddle.

Ines is already waiting for me. She is sitting cross-legged on her bed. She looks even paler in the moonlight. The new girl in the bed next to her is asleep. I can only see her hair. I have a brief pang of jealousy. But Ines's face lights up when she sees me. I am Elly. I'm wearing her clothes, the wig itches on my head. Silently, I extend a hand to Ines. Like sleepwalkers we wander out of the hospital. The porter is watching television. He doesn't see us. No one stops us. Barefoot, we walk along the street. We walk as far as the river and stare at the dark water. A flat barge goes by. Ines remains silent. She doesn't need to say anything. I know it too. She has definitely stood here before, or maybe on another bank. She was holding a girl's hand then too. But she must have returned alone. We don't speak. Ines squeezes my hand. As I make a move towards the bank, she holds me back. I drag her on. I'm stronger than Ines and healthy. She has to follow. The quay wall is high; the black water slaps against it. Over the waves, I hear Ines breathing heavily. She is sniffling. Tears run down her face. I stop just before the edge. My queen dies on this quay. But Ines and I, we stand there. We wait for the sun to come up. It's just her and me. No one else is there.

BELOW ZERO

My sister disappears on a slightly overcast afternoon in June. I imagine how it happens. I see Elly wheeling her bike out of the garage. Her outline is clear and sharp, the background out of focus. She fixes her sports bag to the luggage rack. In it is her judo suit with the green belt. My sister is younger than me. I am thirteen at the time, she is just eleven. We live in a small town. Elly's club meets in a sports hall in the nearest big town. She cycles there on her own across the fields. The wind sweeps through the wheat. From above, it looks like waves on water. Elly stands on the motorway bridge and looks down at the field. The wind ruffles her dark, almost black hair.

I wasn't there. But that's what it must have been like. We always used to stop for a minute up on the top there. We would wave to the long-distance lorry drivers on the motorway, look over at the fields, to the blue peaks of the Taunus mountain range on the horizon. Sometimes we would see a kestrel or a buzzard circling above the fields. Often the cars would come to a standstill under the bridge, a long queue with countless glowing red eyes. A lorry driver would beep his horn: a deep rutting sound. Elly and I used to laugh. We would quickly start pedalling, standing up as we sped off with our bums high in the air, down the cycle path on the other side of the bridge.

The sports hall is in a suburb of Rüsselsheim known as the Grove. I like the name. It sounds so adventurous. The Grove is the area where the workers from the car factory live. In the past, a number of people threw themselves off the top of the high-rise blocks. These days, anyone who wants to kill themselves here drinks themselves to death, or takes an overdose. No one makes a show of suffering any more. These days, the buildings are freshly painted, caretakers tend to the green spaces, keep the hallways clean, remove graffiti. The Grove is flourishing, while the rest of the town declines. Time is running out for cars. Soon, people will be catapulted from town to town by a kind of solar-powered pneumatic tube system. Their souls are left behind though. I read about it in the newspaper.

Our mother went to school in the Grove too, just

like us. But it was a different school back then. Her teachers warned her that if she didn't study hard enough she would end up working on the car assembly line. That was the highest form of punishment when she was young. These days my parents wish they earned as much as the workers on the assembly line. Hamid and Judith both went to university. They never mention it explicitly, but when they talk to each other it's a competition to see who knows better or at least can sound cleverer. My father is an architect, specialising in escalators; my mother writes sustainability reports for large companies. Before my sister and I were born, she worked in an agency. My parents both pore over their computers for hours, their backs hunched. If anyone asks me, I say my parents are freelance. Generally people don't have anything more to say then. Freelance professionals, free from all restrictions and pressures. I think it sounds intimidating. I say it as if it is. I don't like questions. I think of Elly.

Before she disappears on that June afternoon, my sister crosses at the traffic lights on the edge of the Grove. On the opposite side of the junction is the police station. Elly doesn't pay any attention to it. The only sighting of her is at the next set of lights, just before the sports hall. A female witness later recalls seeing my sister, the small, dishevelled girl, with almost black hair, on her red bike. The sports bag falls off Elly's luggage rack right in the middle of the road. Elly flings her bike down at the side of the road and runs back to her bag. My sister is still well and alive when the witness drives on. She quickly loses sight of the girl in her rear-view mirror. She is focused on singing along to a well-known old pop song, very loudly and out of tune. She remembers the song: 'The Eye of the Tiger'. That's the last I hear of my sister. Her trail goes cold here.

The caretaker at the sports hall says he didn't see my sister. The other girls stroll past him. He runs an eye over them. These giggling, long-haired child-women. Hair like whips, silver chains on their teeth, shiny pink nail varnish, denim shorts which barely cover their bums and ripped black tights underneath with holes as big as your head. The caretaker tries not to notice them. The girls whisper among themselves, laugh out loud. They run into the changing room. They leave the door open. They clamber into their judo trousers, tighten the drawstring. My sister would normally be among them. But she is missing. The other girls slip into their stiff jackets with the lapels their opponent has to grab during the fight. They tie their different coloured belts. One by one, the girls enter the dojo with the grey mats on the floor and the mirror on the wall. They form a long line and turn their faces to the instructor. On his command, they all bend first their left knee, then their right. They extend their feet, placing their insteps and big toes one on top of the other. Their knees gape, one fist-width apart, their hands rest on their upper thighs. Their arms hang loosely by the sides of their bodies.

The instructor scans the long line. On the left at the end kneels the girl who has the brown belt already. The other girls have lined up to her right according to the colour of their belts. There are lots of girls with white, yellow, or orange belts. My sister would sit roughly in the middle. But she isn't there. My sister is one of the best in her age group in the club. Her favourite throw is the shoulder throw, seoi-nage. My parents believe the sport will help if anyone attacks her. They chose judo rather than karate because they believe judo to be the more gentle, intelligent sport. Judoka use their opponents' strength against them. They don't attack, they defend themselves. That's what my parents believe. The instructor is in his mid-twenties. He has an angular Viking face. All the girls have a crush on him. They try to fight against him as often as possible. They want him to sweep them to the floor. My sister thinks that's pathetic. She would never submit willingly. The instructor wears a black belt. He studies the girls. Deep in his throat he forms the words. Mukuso, he calls. They all close their eyes. They collect themselves, chase away their thoughts, just for a few seconds. The instructor calls: Rei. He and the girls bow to each other. They pause briefly with their foreheads on the ground. They breathe in the plastic smell of the mats.

Maybe at that moment my sister is already dead. Maybe she is crawling, injured or raped, through some bushes, the branches scratching her cheeks. Tears burn in her eyes, but she is too afraid to make a noise. The attacker's semen drips from her. She is half naked. He is still there, somewhere behind her in the bushes. He is lying in wait. Panic constricts her throat. She knows she can't get away. She is shaking. Her sobs stick in her throat. Something howls. She jumps when she realises it is her. She hurries on, crawling on hands and knees. Then a hand closes round her ankle. My sister kicks out. She defends herself. But the hand slowly pulls her back into the thicket. Maybe it's a gang of youths who surround her in that moment. Maybe it's not one man on his own. Maybe it's several men, or a couple. A woman who lures my sister under a pretext and a man who then drags her onto the back seat of a car. There are so many images, so many stories. It's always a young girl, the main perpetrators are always men. That seems to be the rule. Or maybe nothing actually happened to my sister at all. Maybe she just turned off on her way to the sports hall. Maybe she cycled back or along to the next motorway exit. Her bike is never found either. It disappears like her, without a trace. She hadn't packed anything more than her sports kit. Nothing is missing from her bedroom. No trousers, no skirt, no toothbrush. There is no goodbye letter. We don't get any contact later either. She doesn't call. She doesn't email. It's like my sister is swallowed up by the ground. No one sees her, no one demands a ransom.

My parents and I search for signs of a plan. We want Elly to have simply run away. We want her to be alive somewhere. We cling to that. We often talk about the days prior to her disappearance. The police officers keep asking us about them too. They compare our versions. They question the neighbours. In the majority of cases like this, perpetrators come from the victim's close social circle. First the police suspect my father of having a mistress, then they accuse my mother of having a lover. The investigators speculate that my sister had discovered the new relationship. They insinuate that Elly was disposed of. She probably caught them at it. My parents can hardly speak for rage. They are furious. How could the police suspect them of committing a crime? My mother wants to pour her heart out to a journalist friend. My father urges my mother to keep a clear head. Instead they discuss engaging a private detective and withdraw a sum of money from Elly's savings account, which our grandparents keep topping up. It was meant to be for her education. Even before Elly's disappearance we very rarely received visitors to our house, though more than a dozen of our relatives live in the same small town. When we met them, they would greet us, but Elly and I didn't even nod. We don't know them. Our mother never introduced us. Sometimes my sister and I would go to our school friends' houses for a visit. We never invited them into our playroom. I don't know why. It wasn't as if it was forbidden.

Now my parents and I glide wordlessly past one another. We don't touch, not even in the narrow hallway or in the doorways. My parents don't cry in front of me. Only once do I hear my mother sobbing, behind her closed door. She won't allow herself to cry, because my sister Elly is still alive. That's our rallying cry. We hold fast to it. We know that the likelihood is violence and death. The police search the area with sniffer dogs after a worker at the sewage treatment plant claims to have seen my sister. Later the man is treated for psychosis.

Secretly I picture my sister lifting her bike under the tarpaulins of a truck and getting in the front. This vehicle takes her to France without harm. Travelling like this, Elly reaches the sea. The waves rage, the wind drives the flecks of foam from the spray onto the wet beach. My sister's hair blows in her face. In a shopping centre in the small seaside town on the Atlantic coast she comes across a group of vagrant youths. She follows them obstinately. One boy pelts her with empty cans. But she doesn't give up. When the police come, she flees with the gang. After their getaway together, she belongs to them. During the day she begs with the others, at night she snuggles up to her girlfriend, a French girl, in their army sleeping bag. I hope this girlfriend has her wits about her, is smart enough to know how to break in without getting caught and how to get false papers. This girlfriend looks after Elly, I'm sure of it. My sister's skin has a touch of caramel, summer and winter alike. I am envious of her. Along with her light eyes, the dark soft waves of her hair. When she laughs, her whole body heaves. Laughter bursts out of her. It rocks her. I keep calling to mind the details of her body. But whenever I try to describe Elly in my thoughts, she slips away from me. I can't force her voice into my ear any more. Her face is changing more and more into the one in the photo albums, the unreal face of the prints inside, copied and filed away, slowly fading. Only at night, when I'm asleep, can I see my sister as she is and feel her vitality. In the morning when I wake there are a few precious moments when I don't yet know she has disappeared. Then the memory hits me like a blow.

I collect first moments. Straight after these flashes of light, that's when my forgetting begins. The first time I looked into the eyes of my daughters, Ines and Elly. The first time I met their father. The first time we stepped inside our house. The first time I sat on a school bench. The first time I got a commission. The first time my mother took me to the gynaecologist. The first time. My first time was panting and poking in the dark. I don't know how it happened. I just wanted to prove that I could do it. I acted as if I'd had a hundred men before, slutty and knowing. I rubbed my arse up against Casanova's groin. I was relying on the fact he was still learning the ropes. He didn't notice my blood. He honked his horn as he drove off. I closed the blinds.

The first time I saw Hamid was at a party. A woman was putting a pistol made of porcelain into his hand. He grinned, helplessly, good-naturedly, swinging his other arm, and reached for a glass of red wine. I was convinced he must have three children at home. My red dress was radiant, but I sat quietly in the corner. He didn't notice me. This man is spoken for, I repeated to myself like a catechism. But he didn't look at me. The small woman with the tiger print trousers was eagerly explaining to him how long she had fired the porcelain in the oven and which gallery she was exhibiting in. Hamid smiled politely. He was the only man at the party wearing a suit. The hostess, my dance teacher, was celebrating her birthday. She had invited a random selection of people who were strangers to each other. Perfect for meeting someone in fact. But it didn't work out with Hamid and me. I was too proud and at the same time too shy to talk to him. And what about him? He didn't notice me. After the party I left for France for three months, where I slurped oysters and doubted whether there were any men you could trust these days. My dance teacher had been planning to marry her boyfriend and dance partner a few weeks after her birthday. The wedding was called off. He had threatened to throw himself off the roof. But Hamid and I met each other a second time. It wasn't fate: it was something I cooked up. I thought up a script. I tracked Hamid down on the internet, invited him to view my profile. I revealed that I'd seen him once before and hadn't been able to get him out of my head. I wouldn't have deigned to give any other man so much as an encouraging smile. Hamid reached for the line I had cast. I was responsible. But to friends I would sigh and say it was destiny. We had a second first moment.

First moments are treacherous. You have to stick it out from that moment forth. I seek out first moments, I contrive sensation for myself in my quiet suburban life which is devoid of all unpredictability. I try to picture how wild and determined I was as a young woman. When I catch the spark in Ines's eyes that used to be in mine, I feel old and lifeless. But I can transform myself. For that I need nothing more than make-up and cottage cheese. Both of them make me glow, make my skin smooth. First moments are a matter of perspective. The beginning of the end. The first slug of coffee in the morning. The first time I refused his advances. The first time I tried to switch the phone off, not to pick up the papers any more, to avoid the news. The first time I was drawn back to the data stream, when I tried once again to find Elly on there. Because Elly is now my first and last moment. Elly. My little girl, my wild child, my sanctuary. She's the one. After her, I forgot everything. All the first moments are suddenly just final glimpses, the beginning of the end, harbingers of doom. Elly has gone, disappeared. No one knows what happened to her. There was no demand for ransom, no shoe found, no hair. She cycled to training and she never arrived.

Now I feel my way through the house in the dark. I run my hands over the furniture, the walls, the pictures hanging there. I don't stumble on the stairs. It's the uncertainty which is slowly eating me up. Hamid instructs detectives. He organises action groups and manhunts far and wide. He searches for her in the most remote places, in the most roundabout ways. In vain. Elly is gone. Everything we had goes out of focus, everything we experienced with her falls apart. We are rotting from the inside out. The poison bubbles up until it's in our mouths. Hamid tries to give me hope again. He finds descriptions of persons who match her, he telephones authority after authority. In the end it's always the same answer. Elly has gone. We still have Ines. I hope she stays.

I ask myself whether Elly has run away, whether she couldn't put up with us any longer. I ask myself whether I fought too much with Hamid, whether I was too impatient with Elly, who was contrary, rebellious from an early age. I remember her pinching my upper thigh as a young child. The way she kept pinching me over and over, laughing like an imp, even though I shrieked and scolded her. I remember I ended up digging my fingers into her leg. She barely reached my hips, she was so small. She was shocked to death; she couldn't breathe, her face went red, and only then her features dissolved. A wet baboon mask. When I finally let go, an imprint remained. Elly shouted for her father, her grandparents. But no one was there. And she got no comfort from me.

Now my hair is greasy, stiff with dirt. I slip into the same clothes every day. My fingernails have grown long. They curve. Everyone claims that time heals all wounds, but our time stands still. The pain that I feel doesn't fade. It comes in waves, surges and breaks again, over and over. First it came as a blow. It left me numb for weeks on end. Then senseless anguish, sobbing, collapse. I despise myself, I loathe what is left of my family. I can't change it. I wish I had never become a mother. The danger, the pain, the fear that is wrapped up in motherhood is something I can't bear. There are no more first moments. When your child disappears, everything stops.

I call up beautiful memories to pray myself back to life. I think about Hamid's hands in my lap, his smiling lips; about Ines on the horse, her back straight, her plait dancing on top. I slowly feel my way towards the memories of Elly. As a baby she was neat and long. Soft padded fists, rings of fat on her thighs, a triple chin. But as soon as she docked onto my breasts, she had the force of a truck. She sucked so hard I saw stars. I took pills for the pain, to keep going. On the upside, she could tell night from day by four weeks and she slept through. Apparently that was a huge achievement for a newborn. It meant I could get enough sleep. But rather than relaxing, I kept watch anxiously, in case some calamity might befall her. Was she breathing regularly? Was her stomach swollen or did her nappy need changing? Or was that Ines? I don't know any more. Their baby faces are superimposed on each other. I don't know where one begins and the other ends. Sudden cot death and other macabre afflictions haunted my thoughts. But we were spared. Fear was my constant companion. It is gone now. I no longer look left and right when I cross the street. What else is going to happen to me? Everything seems to be at an end. I try to take care of Ines, to pay attention to her. But I don't seem able to tame my thoughts.

Elly disappeared almost four years ago. With no prior warning. Simply gone, as if she had been put out like a flame. Everyone suspects that we threw her out or killed her. The police investigations took that direction. Perhaps it was just an accident, the officer suggested. As if a confession would burst out of us when faced with her understanding. At home we cursed and raged about these suspicions. But the police clung to them. The distrust against us grew. It spread out, star-shaped.

We saw it in people's eyes in the pharmacy, in the bus driver's slight hesitation when she opened the door for us. The suspicion took root. Even the weather is against us. It's always too cold or too hot. I know I haven't committed a crime. But what was Hamid doing that day? I'm not one hundred per cent sure where he was when. I don't dare ask him. But I pay more attention now. Where he says he's off to, when he comes back. Which female friends he mentions suspiciously infrequently. It wouldn't really affect me if he did cheat on me, or so I imagine. Worse things happen after all. The pain of losing Elly is a fire that never goes out. And even Hamid is standing on the outside, far away, on the other side of the smoke.

After Elly's disappearance I was prescribed pills. I couldn't sleep. But it was the wrong drug. It just made me mushy. It didn't touch the sides. I had to concoct my own mixture to get through the day. Something to make me sleep, something to wake me up, and something for the time in between. I needed to get through it. Sometimes, I can sense that Elly is alive. Then my excitement feels like a wing fluttering inside me. Like individual feathers stroking my diaphragm. I know that it makes no sense to think about her surviving. Elly was so small, so young when she disappeared. But she was old enough to identify any perpetrator, and I don't believe that she ran away. Why would she? It's like I'm living on autopilot. Structure is the only thing holding me up. I keep the tablets in moderation too. Although I've thought more than once that I can't go on. I just want everything to stop. But I still have one daughter. I need to live for her. I need to look after her. I don't go out any more. How could I enjoy myself when my youngest daughter is suffering? How could I dance while she decomposes?

I can't switch off. Without the tablets I would never have managed to carry on. I am infinitely grateful to Big Pharma. Maybe there are a few cases where medication like this did more harm than good. But in actual fact psychopharmaceuticals are a blessing. They have saved my life. Without the pills I would have given up. Maybe I would have jumped, or poisoned myself with exhaust fumes. Or thrown myself under a train. On the internet there are detailed instructions for suicide. You can even buy stud guns. I imagine pressing one of those to my temples. But the risk of it slipping is too great. Then I would probably be permanently paralysed and wouldn't even be able to kill myself. Enough. I will wait for Elly. I can sense she's alive.

My sister is dead. I hardly dare to think it, because I know my belief is enough to kill her. We're all Elly has left. Our belief keeps her alive. Everyone else has given up on her. The police aren't looking for her any more. There are new cases with more promising leads. Elly is being shelved, my father says, raging. He never usually gets angry, but he has hatred in his voice when he talks about the police. I love my father. He looks like an Arab version of Barack Obama. Admittedly he's almost two heads shorter than the former American president, his voice is higher, his smile more shy than winning. But he is a generous, endlessly patient man. My father's father comes from Tunisia. Hamid himself doesn't even speak Arabic. His parents dropped the second language out of consideration for his sister, who has learning difficulties. Sometimes, particularly after Islamist

terrorist attacks, my father likes to insist to strangers
that he is Greek or Spanish. But his name gives him
away immediately. When my sister and I wanted to
tease my father, we would try to pronounce his name
in the Arabic way. First we would pretend to clear our
throat for the guttural H-sound, then we'd spit the
rest of his name out behind it. Just like we had heard
our relatives do when we went on holiday to Tunisia:
Chrrr-amid. It always sounded wrong. We stuck to the
German pronunciation. My mother is the true Arab
in our house. She cooks tagine, chakchoua, couscous,
hangs carpets from the bazaar and camel saddles on the
walls. She cultivates the Arabic heritage that my father
is embarrassed by. Thanks to her, we have the director's
cut of *Lawrence of Arabia* at home. We watch it every
year at Christmas. My mother loves Peter O'Toole in
this role. His blue eyes flashing above the Bedouin scarf.
She would have braved every sandstorm with him. My
father protests that my mother's adoration constitutes
false advertising. After all, Lawrence was actually a Brit.
But my mother argues that he was a true nomad. He
loved the Arabs.

That was all a long time ago. Now Elly skips
through the images on the television, she haunts the
lines of every novel I read. I think I see my sister on
every corner. I've stalked a dozen girls in vain already.

In the meantime, my parents try to make up for the failures of the police. They issue calls for search parties for my sister on the television, via the internet, through every available channel. They give interviews. They allow themselves to be coiffed, powdered, their hair sprayed rigid for the cameras. They look at the blinking red light. They talk into the dark lens. They plead and beg. Even the bishop gives us an audience. But at some point my sister stops being news. She has fizzled out. My parents call the editors, but only their secretaries will speak to them. No one returns their calls. We are alone again. Fear eats away the hours. The clients and agencies that normally employ my mother and father are understanding at first. But when my parents still don't reliably deliver their work six months later, these calls also become infrequent. My parents send me to do the shopping. I'm supposed to pay by card. Sometimes it doesn't work. Then I have to leave the groceries in the supermarket. The checkout operator is annoyed. At home I make apple sauce with rice pudding or pancakes. A sweet, warm comfort food which is meant to fill the void. It doesn't comfort me.

Then I get ill. The doctors operate on me. Suddenly there are only two possibilities, no questions, no compromises any more. Just life or death, zero or one. I savour this clear and simple feeling. My parents also rouse themselves from their stupor. They fuss over me, stuff cushions behind my back, stroke my hair. A girl in the hospital reminds me of my sister. We play with each other. It's wonderful. A feverish warm flowing feeling. When I'm with her there are no questions, no future, also no past. Just a humming present. Almut is small and trusting. We are like sisters. We stick together. We shut the others out. But then she is discharged. She flies off on holiday. When we meet up to play afterwards, Almut acts weirdly. She is wary of me. She looks at me out of the corner of her eye. Every sentence I say, she repeats back as a question: Come on, we'll go out. Shall we go out? I stop calling her. This brief friendship is nothing compared to the eternity in which Elly has disappeared, in which I'm alone with my parents, in which every thought, every action, everything we are revolves solely around my sister.

The neighbour's cat slips through the high grass in our garden right in front of the window. The vegetable patches are full of weeds. The nettles come up to my hips. The fruit falls from the trees. It rots on the ground. Wasps settle on it. The bramble hedge is overgrown. It entwines around the fence, it creeps over the ground, full of thorns. The lawn in the middle is a dusty grey wasteland. The wind whips up the dry sand. It coats my skin. I turn the tap on to attach the hose, but not a drop comes out. The house is crumbling around us. First the bathroom cabinet gets jammed. Then it is hanging off its hinges. Instead of repairing it, my father takes the door off. My mother grumbles at him for that. She is tense, nervous. Her voice trembles, sometimes it topples and breaks off. We have pasta with butter for lunch more and more often, followed by tinned peaches. The fruit swims in the sugary water, orange and slimy. I spear the halves with my fork.

My mother and father get the feeling that my mother's parents blame them for my sister's disappearance. My parents and my grandparents shout at each other. My parents reject my grandparents' apology. The door slams and doesn't open again. My grandparents are banished. My mother makes herself invisible. Her hair hangs over her face. She wears the same dark jumper every day. My father drinks too much. The bags under his eyes swell up. His gaze is dim, then it's furtive, like a lurking crocodile. I stand in front of the mirror and run my finger over my face. I ask myself whether I look good or bad. Even though I know it doesn't make any difference. I reach for the scissors, as if something is compelling me. I cut my hair off. The ends are squint. My parents don't notice. They are too occupied with the search for Elly. I'm not allowed to leave the house on my own at night any more. I'm not allowed to be late, I'm not allowed to get drunk or hang around or get up to no good.

Secretly, I'm angry at my sister. She has taken everything away from me. I have no right to be happy when my sister is suffering, when she might be dead, when she is locked in a cellar, raped, languishing without sunlight or proper food. Elly is gone. That's the only thing that matters. I wish I could run away. But I know that would kill my parents. I want to move away, start again in another place, somewhere where no one knows about my sister. But my parents don't want to go anywhere. They wait in our house, just in case Elly turns up at the door one day. They don't say it out loud, but that's what they are doing. My marks at school, my friends, my birthday — none of it is important. My parents cross off each day in their minds. Sometimes I wake up gasping. My inhaler is lying on my bedside table.

When I'm lying awake at night, I see Elly in her white judo suit. She is running through a red desert. Jagged cliffs tower above her on all sides. She weaves her way through a crack in the rock faces. The dust gives her suit a red tinge. The sun is burning. Elly stares into the light until the sun leaves a black image on her retina. A dark hole in the sky which disintegrates, dazzlingly. My sister is still only eleven. I can't picture her differently. Her hair clings damply to her forehead.

She drags herself up a slope. She is looking for people, water, shelter. But on the top of the mountain there is nothing but the wind which roars in her ears and forces her right up to the edge. My sister's judo jacket is gaping wide open. The white t-shirt underneath is tight against her flat chest. Suddenly a dark blue ink-stain spreads across the left-hand side. As if she has been shot. My sister doesn't take any notice of the stain. She screams wordlessly. Her arms are opened wide. Her hair, the flesh on her cheeks, everything is torn back by the wind. She leans into the storm, which scatters her syllables.

Sometimes I ask myself if this is actually Elly punishing us. What did we do wrong? Judith and I, me and Judith. Judith and the girls. Me next to them. When Elly was still a clump of cells, absolutely tiny, in Judith's belly, I pictured her like Ines. The baby before her. No one is a completely blank page, not even a newborn. But Elly had her own head, her own impish laugh, adorned with dimples. I still believe I didn't know her though. I wish we'd had more time. But there's never time, when all your contracts are about to collapse or spiral out of control. You're the one who pays the price. I put her to bed every evening though. Which book shall I read you? The same one again? Let me tell you a story. The unbridled joy when children discover something new, even if it's only a loose cable swinging, or perforated light falling through a sieve. The happiness when they nestle into you, beg for a story, their eyes hanging on your every word, and you know: everything you say will come true. That's a gift that only children possess. They make everything real. Judith and I are no longer children. We are full of fears and worries. There is no salvation any more, not even the little death. We hold back. It's not everyday life that eats us up, but a tiny moment of distraction. A brief instant in which we weren't paying attention, and our youngest daughter disappeared. I blame myself because we didn't give her a lift to training. But it was the same route that she went to school. She cycled it daily on her bike by herself. What tortures me even more is the question of whether Elly might actually have begun to disappear much earlier? What if we just didn't notice?

The police officer asks whether Elly has run away before. Judith and I shake our heads. No drugs, no signs of mental illness. No one in our house is violent. Can a child who grows up in affluent circumstances still go off the rails? There are countless books with explanations. Parenting guides, psychoanalytical models. I don't want to read these books. But I can't stop myself. The police officer says there are two possibilities if children aren't found within twenty-four hours: either they may be victim of a violent crime, or they don't want to be found.

Our stools squeak as we push them together to form a circle. Hamid is skiving off. The other parents have mostly turned up in couples. Blurry images hang on the walls, a box of tissues is lying on a side table. We go round in a circle, telling stories of the loss of our children. I am the only one without a grave. I place all my hopes on the woman with a large tattoo on her forearm. I scoot to the edge of my stool to be near her. The course leader has asked her to speak. The tattooed woman is meant to take on her partner's role. She responds dutifully. Her voice squeaks. Disappointed, I lean back again. I wish my friend the dancer were here. She once told me how she sniffed cocaine before a PTA meeting so she could cope with the discussions about organic peas and carrots, or buying gift vouchers for the teaching assistants. I told her to give that stuff a rest. In fact I was always envious of her audacity. Of the unrelenting way she continued to flog her body in search of adventure. Later, she moved to the country. Now when we meet up, we try not to touch on the old times at all, the long nights, the parties and the men we shared. I got Hamid and the girls. My friend shears sheep now, she rides horses and makes jelly. That's so much more satisfying, she says, and I contemplate the deep smile lines between her nose and mouth. I, on the other hand, think I've hardly changed in the last twenty years. My dress from my school leavers' do still fits me. The mourners in the circle of stools are looking at me expectantly. I'm supposed to share something. Quickly I say: I would trade my life for my daughter's. I feel heroic. The tattooed woman nods approvingly. But I know how hollow my words are. The psychologist who runs the circle of stools winks at me. Or maybe it's just a nervous tick. The shutters come down. I don't finish my sentences. But the course leader nods encouragingly at me. She asks what my name is again. I scream in her face with my silence. I want everything and so much more. Anything but pity. I leave.

Outside, raindrops dampen my face. A fighter jet breaks the sound barrier; afterwards, hush falls over the sparrows in the trees. It is deathly still. As if something has sucked up every sound. A storm is about to break.

There is rumbling behind the clouds. A gust of wind sends a plastic bag swirling. It spirals up into the sky.

The point is, I've got a grip on myself. And that helps me now as well as before. There are people who can't even take nasal spray. They get addicted immediately. People like that have no limits. It doesn't make the slightest difference whether it's pills, coffee, drugs, or chocolate. They just can't stop. I'm not like that. Everything in moderation. Everything according to plan. A routine set in stone. That's the secret. That's how I do it. Two children and a husband, and on top of that a job with a high degree of responsibility and the prospect of good earnings if you are clever about it. Always take it slowly, don't overdo it, and only cut loose at the weekend.

By the age of twenty I had started training as a radiographer. Although I had the grades for university, I didn't feel confident enough to go yet. My parents ran a manual business. University was something alien to me. So after school I spent three years fastening lead aprons round other people. My colleague at the hospital suggested I try something from the drugs cabinet. At first I declined. A few weeks later we went on a night out together and he was raving again about how exceptional the high was. I read the package insert from his pills. There was nothing dramatic in it — at most heart arrhythmia. At the time I thought: I live such a healthy and boring life, I floss and wear a helmet when I cycle, I can take this risk for once. Then at least I'll know what it feels like. The pills were antiepileptics, I think. The colleague who gave them to me was a paramedic. I knew that in an emergency he'd revive me. But he didn't need to. I was completely absent, yet completely present at the same time. I was floating in the corner of the room and I could see myself. As if I was my own participant observer. My thoughts flashed, sharp like razors. I kept thinking I should write them down, they were so brilliant. But they flew away as quickly as they came. My whole body pulsated with sensations. They streamed from my fingertips, colouring my surroundings like on an infrared camera. Normally strangers stress me out, and we were in a bar. But thanks to the pills everyone was my friend. The practical thing about pills is they aren't drugs, they are still medicine. So the high feels like a cure. Take this now and you'll feel better. You persuade yourself that they are only marginally more dangerous than vitamins. Yet part of the rush lies in the fact that you know how much higher the risk is. The pills cured me of shyness. Right from that very first time all my inhibitions were gone. I wasn't a nymphomaniac. I was completely in control, crystal clear, and my skin was so sensitive it was untrue. Even the covers on the sofa turned me on. We were sitting on velvet with wide ribbing. My companion grinned, and we went back to his place. It was the best sex of my life. Unfortunately the bloke was an idiot. But he was attractive, and thanks to the pills, he more than hit the spot. Even the sofa would probably have done it for me that night. I was glowing, sparkling, from the inside out. A wick was burning inside of me, consuming my wax. The next day I was completely empty. But I didn't have a hangover.

By the age of thirty, I was married with two children. That suited me. One step at a time. What I did at the weekend, when my husband was watching the children, was nobody's business. During the week I didn't get a minute to myself. There was always something. Children are great, but they are utter dictators. There's no time out, no breaks, they are always on the ball. My husband doesn't take anything. I know that. Alcohol at most. He is so laidback it's untrue. He can drink three pots of coffee and sleep like a baby afterwards. It took me ten years before I stopped getting palpitations and pixelated vision from caffeine. My husband travels a lot for work; he's an architect. The escalators he designs are often in far-flung towns. He's usually a lone soldier in the army of builders working on the train stations, department stores, and shopping malls of this world. I think he loves escalators because they transport people like goods, going up or down, to heaven or hell. Escalators are like gods. People are at their mercy. At any rate, Hamid is always on the move, staying in workers' hostels or other dives. I never asked him what he did during the week. But I got Saturday evenings off in return. Then I would hit the town with the girls, and sometimes with a bloke from the internet. I started to hook up with them when I was annoyed with my husband. It was more exciting than it was enjoyable: I didn't know the men very well. I would take something to stay awake and something to relax, with a vodka chaser. That doesn't give you a headache. Really good spirits don't burn either. They are very soft, sort of oily on your tongue. I would never offer the blokes pills or anything else. That was their lookout. When there were strangers around, I would be careful. I never took new substances then. Nothing bad ever happened to me mind you, but — touch wood — that's how I wanted it to stay. One step at a time.

These days I earn my money writing sustainability reports for a range of companies. After the children arrived, I went freelance. It's just better if you can be flexible. With two children, there's always one that is ill, falls off the climbing frame or has an appointment with the speech therapist. Sustainability is the market of the future. Ethical economies. Profit in proportion.

Thinking socially and ecologically, and taking on corporate social responsibility as a company and actively working towards this goal. This is the only way that businesses today can set themselves up as future oriented. This is what it's about after all: conserving resources for the next generation, discovering how we can all get along with each other and live in prosperity. More and more people have an eye for this when shopping: how does this or that brand treat its workers and how do they remunerate the producers, say in third world countries. Are the products ecologically sustainable and fair trade? Does the transport or production consume unnecessary amounts of energy? The same goes for services, more or less. These are all the aspects I have to take into account in my reports. But I'm only repackaging it. I don't create the content. The firms themselves supply it. I just turn it into comprehensible texts. It's pretty banal, what I do, in the end. I don't know what the point was of studying for this. But since Elly disappeared, my studies don't help any more. Every sentence just consists of disconnected words. The words disintegrate into syllables. Sometimes I stare at a letter or the blinking cursor for minutes at a time. Only my little pink friends can help me then. I swallow them. They pick me up.

ELLY

My sister has been gone a long time. It was four years ago this Thursday. I am older now. It won't be long before I'm an adult. I long for that every day. But I'm still not allowed to go out without telling my parents. Sometimes I climb up the hunter's lookout in the woods with the elder of the two boys from next door. We lie in wait, and when a deer appears in the clearing we press our faces up to the slit in between the boards. We make use of those few seconds to lean our shoulders softly against each other or to let a finger sidle up to the other's hand. I can feel the boy's warmth. He smells of hay. When I've finished school, I want to go to Australia to be an au pair. I practise sometimes with the boy next door's younger brother. He can't remember my sister. He was too young at the time. I love him for that. I bury my nose in his fine, almost white hair. His hands are plump. I put chocolate coins in them. Then the phone rings. It rings inside me. The sound is shrill. It vibrates in my skull. I turn hot, then cold. The ground opens up.

The phone rings. My trainers are outside on the terrace getting drenched by the rain. I'm staring out of the window while I peel potatoes. I still need to practise for a vocab test, so I'm peeling them in a hurry. The telephone doesn't stop ringing. The sound seems to be getting louder and louder. It echoes. The knife slips. Blood pours from my thumb. My mother beckons me to answer the phone. She doesn't want to speak to anyone. I lie and say she isn't in. I'm sucking the blood from my cut when the female police officer on the other end of the line says: We have found a person who fits the description of your sister. Other officials have said something similar a few times before. It was always a false alarm. But this time it's different. My parents are speechless when I tell them.

The voice on the telephone says the person concerned is a girl aged approximately fifteen years old. Not very tall, thin, with shaggy dark, almost black, hair. She was found lying in between beach huts at a Danish seaside resort. The beach was deserted at the time, back in October; the huts there were locked up. Gulls circled above the foamy sea. A few cars were parked in the street by the beach. The owners didn't get out, they just reclined their seats, and closed their eyes or stared at the sea through the windscreen. One of these parked-up drivers discovered the girl. She was wearing a black binbag over her clothes, probably to keep out the damp. She had built a camp behind the huts on a set of tyres. She didn't say anything when the man spoke to her. She immediately tried to hit him with an iron bar. He managed to restrain her. Soon police officers and youth workers were on the spot. The young girl didn't speak. She babbled. She attacked everyone.

The police took her to the hospital. The doctors there didn't rush her, they observed her, worked by instinct. The girl cowered in the corner of the treatment room. She even relieved herself there. She hardly touched the food they brought. The doctors didn't get any response from her for days. Eventually they took the girl to supported housing. A young female doctor would come and sit next to the girl. Every day she got a bit closer. At first the girl hid behind her chair and snarled. After five days she accepted the doctor's presence. The girl didn't do much during the hours the doctor sat there with her. She rocked back and forth or pulled strands of hair over her face and contemplated the ends. Sometimes she would bite her nails a bit or scratch the crook of her elbow. The doctor felt sorry for the girl. She put her in mind of a frightened animal. But the girl knows how to write, so they discovered after several weeks. A police officer called round various aid organisations and eventually ended up comparing the girl with Elly's picture. Our telephone rang.

My parents say it's impossible. This girl can't be our daughter. There must be some mistake. They try to compose themselves. The prospect is too enticing. We can't get our hopes up; it takes too much out of us. We can't cope with another disappointment. It's better to assume the worst. Our vocal chords rasp. We clear our throats. But the lump is too low down. We can't shift it. We discuss which one of us should fly to Denmark. In the end both my parents go. They book separate flights in case there is a crash. I am supposed to carry on going to school like nothing has happened.

My mother has frozen meals for me. Every day I heat up the contents of one of the Tupperware tubs. The block of brown ice turns into goulash, the red one into tomato soup. I spoon the food from the tub and wipe it out with a slice of bread. I don't tell anyone about the phone call. Then everything would come true. I don't believe in miracles. I try to put one foot in front of the other. I get through the day bit by bit. By the evening I can no longer remember what I did in the morning. I watch TV until the sun comes up again. I can't sleep. Something tingles under my tailbone, I can't switch off. I run through the woods to tire myself out. I go as fast as I can. I gasp, my blood thunders in my ears. The treetops above me are spinning. I trip over a root. My chin splits open. I can smell moss. Pine needles stick to my face. My mother's voice pounds in my head. She says: It's true. We've got her back. It's unbelievable. I ask Judith if she is really sure. My mother flies into a rage and tries to cut me off, but then she interrupts herself and says I'll see soon enough. They will be coming back with Elly the day after tomorrow. I knock my trainers together.

The nose of the aeroplane icon is pointing down. I'm standing behind the stainless-steel barriers where I alternate between staring at the sliding door and staring at my watch again. Every few seconds the door glides to one side, releasing bunches of people with their suitcases on wheels and their baggage carts. Over the tannoy, passengers with foreign-sounding names are requested to make their way to their flight. Outside on the apron a mobile stairway docks onto an Airbus. Then the sliding door made of opaque glass glides to one side. I see my parents first. They are pushing a baggage cart. A girl is sitting on top of the cases. That must be my sister. I don't recognise her. She has pulled the hood of her sweater up and is wearing sunglasses. I can't even make out her figure. Her jacket and trousers swamp her.

Then suddenly there are flashes. Photographers jump in front of the baggage cart, shouting loudly, gesticulating. One even reaches for her hood, but Elly clutches it tightly with both hands. My father takes my hand and pulls me away. We flee from the photographers. We run through the airport. The crowd parts before us. We're on the motorway before we shake the press off. I ask my mother whether her former colleagues might have got wind of the arrival time from her? She had a spell as a reporter many years ago. She shakes her head. I can tell by her cheeks that she is clenching her teeth. I squint at Elly, who is sitting next to me on the back seat. She has taken her sunglasses off. I don't know what I am supposed to say. So I say: I'm glad that you're back again. Elly looks at me, but I don't recognise her. She looks older than fifteen. Her skin is taut over her pointed chin. It is wrinkled around her eyes. Don't be scared, my mother said on the phone. She has had terrible experiences. They have changed her. The Elly I know has been extinguished. I don't like it. The new Elly next to me looks tired and tense at the same time. One hand is resting on the door handle. As if she wants to jump out of the moving car. I stare silently out of the window on the other side.

My parents and I observe Elly like an animal at the zoo. An invisible pane of glass separates her from us.

Elly remains deadened, turned in on herself. She doesn't tell us anything about her life in the past four years. Our parents know the story from the doctors. They suspect that Elly had been kept captive in a cell, without light, with very little food or water, deliberate abuse. Perhaps there was more than one captor, perhaps she was passed around or sold. In any case she is severely traumatised. The assessor prescribes complete rest and recuperation. No loud noises, no physical contact, no pressure. I feel guilty for seeing her tormented. It's as if I'd betrayed my sister with my thoughts, as if I'd brought her to it. But I didn't do anything. That's what my parents reproach themselves for: for not doing anything. I was still a child when my sister disappeared. My memory is unreliable. My mother and my father are happy that we have Elly back again.

I keep looking at my newly returned sister. Her thin hair, the parchment colour of her skin, the way she splays her little finger when she holds her fork. She moves around the edges of the rooms. The middle is uncomfortable for her. I guess she is afraid of feeling exposed there. She cuts corners so fine that her sleeve sometimes gets caught on the door handle. I tell her that I don't play tennis any more, or do athletics or trampolining. I don't mention judo. It doesn't feel appropriate. I don't do any sport any more, apart from shopping. Without spending any money. That's also very strenuous, I claim. Elly nods. She is trying to find an American radio station on the internet. She refuses my help. Finally the sound of a drawling presenter in bubblegum American, followed by a thumping pop song with a female singer whose voice keeps breaking. Elly listens to American college radio. I ask her how she knows the station. She shrugs her shoulders and says everyone knows it. I follow her gaze to the shelves on the wall. The two blue vases are standing there, presents from our grandparents. Elly points to them. Laurel and Hardy, she says, and laughs. One vase has a long neck, the other is spherical. I use the vases as hand puppets. Mirror, mirror, on the wall. Who's the fairest of them all? I nudge Elly with the neck of the vase. She purses her mouth. That's so babyish, she says. But I don't back down. I repeat the phrase. Eventually she sighs: Stop this nonsense. Before she would have tickled me into submission or declared that she was the fairest of them all, and we would have strutted around in front of the mirror for an imaginary casting. An electric sander screams into life in the garden next door. Our neighbour is bending over the window frames he has taken out. He is wearing a dust mask. The shavings fly up into the air. The draughts threaten to rip the papers from the pinboard. Elly asks me to shut the window. I briefly consider refusing, then stand up. The sander sounds quieter but isn't completely silenced. Elly is shivering. I tell her it will definitely be warmer tomorrow. I persuade her to come for a walk. She trudges alongside me with her head bowed. Before she practically used to bounce. She has hardly grown in the past four years, but her hands are old. There's not much more to see of her. The new Elly covers herself up. Even at home she never takes off her hoodie. When our mother creeps into her room at night to stuff the sweater in the washing machine, Elly wakes up immediately. Guiltily, our mother puts the hoodie back. After that Elly doesn't even take it off at night any more.

My younger daughter is back. I still can't quite believe it, I tell my friend from the radio. She nods encouragingly and brings the microphone closer to my face. I clear my throat, swallow. The clock ticks. The corners of my mouth are cracked. Probably due to the smiling. What kind of feeling was it when you saw Elly again for the first time? My friend's voice sounds unctuous. It is dripping with compassion. I was scared, I say. My voice goes up at the end of the sentence. I'm almost asking a question. In actual fact I don't remember my feelings. I see Elly before me, as she enters the bare room. The way she gazes at the floor, hardly daring to look Hamid and me in the eyes. He squeezes my hand. I am rooted to the spot. Elly has completely changed. She slides along the wall like a shadow. Thin, pale, her hands shaking. I had never seen her so anxious before.

But I knew: that's my child. I growl the sentence. My friend's eyes open wide. That's what she wanted to hear. I bet she is mentally making a note of this point for a cut in the recording. She bites her lips. Did you not hesitate even for a moment? No, I say, not for a moment. I didn't need a blood test to know. Quite the opposite, I was ashamed of myself for doubting during the years she had disappeared. For believing she was dead. I regret that. She is alive. She is so incredibly resilient. I'm proud of her. She is fighting her way back into her life right now. Of course we are trying to help her. But it's not easy to put yourself in her place. The hardest thing for me is leaving her in peace. Obviously we're not going to throw a party for her. I'm clear on that. But finding the right tone of voice to wrench her out of the void when her gaze drifts off, that's not easy. My friend nods. She has children of her own. I can't convey to her quite how far removed my Elly is from them. After the interview I am completely exhausted. Back at home I open the windows and the door to the terrace. The wind blasts through the house. I knock on Elly's door and open it at the same time. Elly is sitting on the edge of the bed. It looks uncomfortable. As if she is expecting to be taken away any minute. I'm so shocked I can't get a word out. She is here. She is really here. We look at each other, and it's Elly who comes and huddles into me. I hesitate, then place my hand on her ribs. I can feel them even through the thick hoodie. Her breath goes in and out.

Sometimes I try to remember how we were before. How my sister and I used to play, the way I would tell her who she was: Little Red Riding Hood, the kraken, Pluto the hellhound, Peter the Stork. The way she followed me everywhere, and only occasionally refused to play along. The way we threw the apples to the horses in the meadow, but neither of us ever admitted that we were too cowardly to offer them on our outstretched hand.

I was the big sister, and even on holiday I told Elly what to do and what not to do. We built dens out of branches and went to sleep in them. Our parents only found us after the sun had gone down. Back then they weren't concerned, just amused. They spent half the day dozing on sun loungers in the garden. Our mother would flick through a magazine, while our father stared into space. He was happy like that. Just being there. I think he was listening to the birds, the horses snorting, watching them chase away midges by twitching their bodies or flicking their tails. In the afternoon he would get up and make limeade from sugar, soda water, and lime. There was no shop. The village consisted of a single long strip of road with no asphalt, more like a sandy track with cobblestones in places. Prettily restored farmers' cottages with timber frames and chickens behind fences. Beyond that nothing but forest. We rarely caught sight of the residents. We kept to ourselves. One time, my sister and I found cockchafer larvae in the ground, thick white grubs. We dug them out and put them in a jam jar, screwed the lid on tight. Every day we looked at them. Then we opened the jar, because we were afraid the creatures might die. But when the cockchafers finally hatched, we weren't there to see it. They flew away without us. The family we were back then doesn't exist any more. Even now Elly has returned, nothing will go back to the way it was before.

Back then, Elly and I used to act out the Greek myths too. She was Zeus and I was Europa, who allows herself to be abducted by the father of the gods disguised as a bull. Those stories are taboo now. They are all far too gruesome. My parents turn the television off when the news comes on. They don't watch crime series any more. They get rid of everything which could remind Elly of her captivity. There are no keys in our house any more. All the doors stay open. We don't go to the zoo, because the animals there are locked up. We avoid petrol stations with missing person posters; if my father catches sight of a flyer, he keeps on driving. If Elly so much as coughs, my parents rush her to the doctor. They insist on staying in the room during the examination.

Elly doesn't have to go to school yet. Our parents are looking after her at home. But it's open season now. The police would like to interview Elly. They want to investigate the criminals who abducted Elly. She shakes her head. We can see that she still feels threatened. Sometimes a sentence escapes her, an attempt at conversation. Her voice sounds strange, bruised. It takes a long time for her to thaw even slightly. Eventually she forces herself. Comes to join us at the table, on the sofa or the terrace. We show her photo albums and ask if she remembers. Do you remember when? In the theme park, when the dolphin pulled you along in a boat. When you forgot your bag on the first day of school. When you scratched the chicken pox until it bled. When we were all happy. Elly listens, sometimes she even asks questions. She asks whether Granny is still such a crosspatch, and whether Grandad is well. She asks what her friends are up to, what happened to the neighbour's cat. Eventually our grandparents come for a visit too. Our grandfather immediately hugs Elly. She stands there stiffly and allows it to happen. He holds Elly's hand and talks about her birthday five years ago. Elly smiles behind her sunglasses and listens to him attentively. Our grandmother stays in the background. She watches Elly carefully, but doesn't approach her. Eventually she shakes her hand formally. Our mother pulls her mother into the kitchen. I hear her hissing in there. Our grandmother retaliates. She says: Have you lost your minds? That's not your child. Our mother throws our grandparents out. Grandad is sad. Afterwards we play cards. Elly lets us win once each. Our father notices and admonishes her gently. Elly looks at him in horror and leaves the table. My sister always used to fight until the last card, the very last trick. She used to be mortally offended when I won. Our father repeats the mantra that Elly has changed. Something doesn't feel right to me.

Judith is lying next to me in bed. She undressed in silence, pulled on her short nightdress, and rolled under the covers without even glancing at me. She is holding it together. I understand. Everything is too much right now. Elly is back. We ought to be cheering and celebrating. But in fact it's exhausting. It's like it is with a newborn. We all have to get used to one another first. Elly is much more than four years removed from us. Judith says we shouldn't ask too much of ourselves. We can't go back to being familiar and intimate just like that. Apparently that applies to us as a couple too. Judith acts like we're down a mine and she is bone tired. Frankly it's ridiculous. What, if you please, could be so difficult and exhausting between us, now that Elly is back? I try to get Judith to relax with wine. I massage her neck, put her feet up. Nothing is right. Even if I hold my breath next

87

to her on the mattress it's too much for her. We share a duvet, a mattress. There is no partition in our bed. It ought to be so easy to move over in the other person's direction, to rekindle the old warmth. But it's as if we're holed up in the same room conducting a long-distance relationship. At first I still reached for Judith, I would put my arm round her hips in the kitchen, gently kiss her ear. If she blinked anxiously or began to manically unload the dishwasher, I would quickly step away. Have I changed? Does my breath smell? Or my fat wobble? Is that all it is? I try to pull myself together. Sulking is childish. In any case, there are more important issues. Judith is right: we need to protect Elly. Nothing must ever happen to her again. We wrap her in cotton wool, we mollycoddle her. I'm not sure whether she enjoys these ministrations. At times I get the impression my youngest daughter is much older than she is. But then again there are things she doesn't know that every other girl her age does. She was away for too long. The police psychologist advised us that Elly shouldn't stay with us to begin with. Being near us might be too much for her. Judith didn't take the suggestion on board. I thought we should have talked about it. But that's what she's like: Judith makes decisions on her own, then together we have to bear the consequences. I used to like the fact that she always takes the lead. Now I fear her harsh judgement. The flipside is that I can trust Judith. Two hundred per cent. She stands by her man. I disappear behind her. Judith would say I push her to the front. She grunts to indicate I should turn the bedside lamp off. But I want to look at her for a moment longer. The way she tosses and turns in the attempt to drift off. Her fists clenched around the duvet. Her closed eyelids with their blue veins. Darling, I murmur. Her eyeballs stop rolling for a second, her lids stay tightly shut. Guiltily, I think of all the things I didn't accomplish today. It's a long list. Every day it gets longer. As long as it's light I procrastinate. I lose myself in a thousand trivial tasks, flit from one thing to another in my office or doing chores. I can't even sit still in the evening when I try to reward myself for my day's work with wine or snacks. It's only when I lie down that the list catches up with me and stops me going to sleep. Elly is back. Our greatest desire has been fulfilled. Now everyday life can begin. We are trying to make everything right again. I think I'll start with the washing up.

My mother bustles around the house. I'm not allowed to sit still either. I have to tidy up for Elly, fetch things or take them away again. Everything is supposed to be lovely, perfect. Nothing can ever get out of control again.

I hurry through the shopping centre in the shade of the concrete roof. The smell of piss by the shopping trolleys, squashed strawberries lying on the ground, a child crawling in front of the kebab van. I need to get butter, cherries, and sausages. I have no imagination when it comes to meat, what tastes good, what's the least bad for you. It all seems poisonous to me. My glass is always half empty these days. I don't believe in cures, or promises.

Elly is back at school. My parents wanted to stop her. They said it was too soon. But Elly seems to be the old stubborn Elly again. She insists. She joined a different year group, in a different school. To avoid awkward questions. But everyone in our area knows the story. They stare at Elly behind her back. The unasked questions bore holes in her skin, but she doesn't seem to notice. Elly hunches over her workbook diligently. She is always doing extra work. If there are three exercises set for homework, she'll do eight. She revises for class tests late into the night. Her average mark is nearly one hundred per cent. Before she disappeared, Elly tended to be lazy. Now she has a go at me if I smudge my books. She soaks up vocabulary or formulas, even names and the anecdotes that go with them, like a sponge. I am amazed at her memory. She never forgets a birthday or which girl hasn't been class representative yet, who got the worst marks in PE and who doesn't tie their shoe-laces. Before she was more of a loner. She never used to join in the Mother May I games the other girls played. Now she commits relationships and moods to memory, as swiftly and permanently as a camera. She always knows who went out with whom. She can usually also predict the next pairing. The new Elly is a social oracle. She knows the invisible ties that bind people, the powers of attraction and repulsion. Elly is the buffer in the middle, she uses her foolproof intuition to bring every conflict back into harmony. Quietly and without a fuss, she mends the rifts between friends. She speaks first to one, then the other, brings them back together again. Her schoolmates are impressed by this new Elly. I find her gift unnerving. Maybe this ability was her only chance of survival in the cellar? I can't imagine lasting a single day in captivity like that. I admire my sister's strength.

Elly's class are learning a dance for the school play. The teacher shows them a video of an old Madonna hit. None of the students know the song. It's a long time since it was at the top of the charts. While it's playing, Elly sings along. Her lips move in time with the singer's, she copies her dramatic gestures and movements like a mirror. She writhes in theatrical agony and sings about a hard lesson she had to learn. She claims she was a fortress that her lover in the video had to burn. That pain is a warning that something is wrong, and she prays that it won't be long. She has barely stopped singing before applause breaks out. Elly gives a little curtsey. Smiling, she bows her head. She is enjoying the ovation.

But at home Elly remains shut tight like an oyster. Our parents and I hold our breath so my sister can catch hers. I rebuke myself for the fact she doesn't live up to my expectations of her. When I was younger I could bend everything into the shape I wanted. I could even declare that girl Almut was Elly. That doesn't work any more. I needed to learn that I couldn't dictate every-thing. Elly was my hardest lesson. I'm really making an effort now. Then Elly has a go at me when I accidentally use her toothbrush. She acts as if I threatened her with a machine gun. I say: Calm down. I'll get you a new toothbrush. But she doesn't want to calm down. She hisses and spits, works herself up. Her accusations grow more and more fanciful. She claims I never liked her. That she had deposed me, the first born, from the parental throne. That I had never forgiven her for it. I say nothing, because the more I say, the angrier she gets. It is as if she has been waiting for an opportunity to explode. Our father hears the screaming in the bath-room. He wants to soothe Elly. But the minute she sees him she bellows. Wordlessly. Like a bull. We stare at her in horror. She hammers on the tiles. Our father wraps his arms round her, she tears herself free. Breathlessly she blurts out that she does actually want to speak to the police now. Our father says she should calm down first. Elly just snorts. He is adamant that Elly doesn't need to force herself to do it. That it is bound to be very painful for her. That she doesn't have to summon up these experiences again. But Elly wants to. She says she wants to prevent the same thing happening to others. Later, our mother praises Elly for being very brave. Every day for a week, my sister travels to the police station with an officer. Elly's eyes stare into space, her hands tremble. But when she comes back home to us on the first day of the police questioning, it's the officer who is in shock. Elly looks relieved. She has told the story of her captivity. Now the officer knows all the gruesome details. Because of the ongoing investigation, Elly is sworn to silence, although she couldn't name any names, any places, any dates anyway. There were other girls there. The officer has seen the brands on Elly's body where cigarettes were stubbed out. Her back is covered with scars. Elly says that the perpetrators tried to change her external appearance. That they bleached her hair. Constant hunger apparently restricted her growth, and even made the curls fall out of her hair. They also broke her nose several times. The X-ray verifies her testimony. The officer doesn't dare to ask about rape straight away. She tries to keep her composure. But Elly's testimony weighs heavy on her chest. The anxiety sits deep. After the interview is over, the officer suggests that Elly see a trauma expert. Even if she appears incredibly strong, she says my sister needs support on her journey back to normality. Elly and our parents agree. Our mother and our father want to do everything right. The police officer drives Elly to the therapist.

Less than two hours later, the phone rings. The therapist is calling from the clinic. At first our mother doesn't understand what the woman wants. What's wrong with this photo? What are you trying to say? she asks. The therapist is clearly talking about an old holiday photo of us. A tourist snapped it for us on the beach. We are laughing and saying 'cheesecake' so our smiles are nice and wide. But the therapist isn't interested in that. She wants to talk about Elly's ears. They are easy to make out on the photo. The therapist says: The girl you sent to me can't be your daughter, it's impossible. She asks my mother to compare the ears on the photo with Elly's ears. Do you see the earlobes? They are completely different. The whole outer form of the ear, even the folds leading to the ear canal, are shaped differently. Some things don't change, the therapist says. Our mother is silent. The therapist continues: Don't come and collect her. We'll put her up on our children's ward for now, though she is most likely a lot older than your daughter. But until we have proof of her real age and identity, you will still be her legal guardians. Do you agree? The colour drains from my mother's face. She says nothing. The therapist repeats it once more: This girl is not your daughter. We don't know who she is. She could be dangerous. At the very least she is a liar. My mother is silent. The therapist says: I know that's too much for you to take in right now. You don't need to make any arrangements. We'll take care of it. Please, leave her here in the clinic. My mother moans: Okay. She hangs up. My father furrows his brow. He asks whether that was really the therapist on the phone? How does my mother know that the voice didn't belong to an imposter? My mother bursts out laughing. She immediately clamps her hand over her mouth. Laughing is completely inappropriate right now. My father asks: What shall we do? My mother says in a monotone: None of this can be true. Then she thinks better of it. She says: This isn't happening. We have to pick her up. She reaches for the car key.

We drive to the clinic together. The therapist's eyebrows travel up to her hairline. But she doesn't mention her suspicions in Elly's presence. They don't stop us taking my sister. Elly's arms are wrapped around her upper body. She gets into our car. The headlights cut through the darkness. The cat's eyes on the side of the road whizz past. My father says: They're driving us all mad. It's not clear who he is talking about. He suggests we go south. My mother is sitting at the wheel. She asks over her shoulder: Elly, are you still awake?

On the island there's no mobile signal. Nothing but birds and rabbits. But the sea is overflowing with life. An abundance of fish, plankton, sea urchins, starfish. Whole forests of seaweed waving underwater. Individual fronds wash up on the beach. The island lies in the outlet from the bay. It resembles a large grey ramp. At the highest point, a granite cliff drops steeply into the sea. The slope on the other side, covered by thin grass, tapers to a sandy spit of land. I found accommodation for Judith, the girls, and myself in a former goat shed at the foot of the flat-topped hill. We're safe here. The island is privately owned. I know the owner from a job. He won the island in a game of skat years ago. This year a prince is living in the villa with the high walls. We don't see him. We only meet the two bodyguards with their machine guns who are housed in the other half of the goat shed. They greet us in friendly fashion. We nod in return. Judith's face is still furious. She's probably sulking about the water. It hasn't rained for weeks. What little water there is on the island is earmarked for the prince. We have to haul our drinking water in huge gallons from the mainland. Our inflatable dinghy sinks noticeably lower under the weight. With the help of the outboard motor it rattles over the water, it cuts through the waves in the steel-grey sea. The bow hops up and down. Judith and the girls hold on to the ropes. Judith's chest heaves under her bikini straps.

I rinse my coffee cup with the water left over from cleaning my teeth. In the former goat shed even the toilet doesn't flush. When we can't get the stench out of our noses any more — sometimes we leave it a whole day — I tip a bucket of water that's been re-used multiple times down the pan. We don't shower at all. Salt crystals form on my skin, dull and rough; the skin on my lips bursts open. When I'm alone, I suck on my arm, like deer suck on salt blocks in the snow. A gull shrieks. Elly scurries over to me in the kitchen. I don't look up. I offer her something to drink. She shakes her head. We settle down in the shade on the veranda. She fans herself with a rolled-up newspaper. We try to move as little as possible. My white shirt is freshly ironed. It is tight across my chest. Every morning I pump up my pecs with purposeful, vigorous press-ups. Then I shave my cheeks and while I do, I contemplate my tanned brown, clear-cut face. My face is the reason that if I'm standing at a junction with a hundred other people, the eyes of the disoriented tourists are guaranteed to turn in my direction, just as surely as the needle on a compass points north. Deferentially, they hold their open guide books out to me and ask the way. As if I ever know. I'm forever getting lost because my thoughts stray from the path, because the infinite flux of possibilities doesn't allow me to concentrate on zebra crossings, street names and alleyways, traffic lights, anything that could tell me the direction. I'm a simpleton who looks like a good shepherd. The strangers on the street see my clear face, my ironed shirt, my taut muscles, and in their eyes that makes me the hero who will lead them out of the labyrinth. I know that my eyes give me away. That's why I wear the darkest sunglasses you can buy. My mop of hair is combed smooth, rigid with gel. The hair on my chest is short and neat. I stride over the jagged stones towards the jetty. Once I'm there I position myself next to Judith's head and start talking into thin air. I don't wait for a response. I talk to kill time, otherwise questions will start flying. I spot Elly, who has followed me. Now she groans loudly. She says she can't bear the heat any more. Before, Elly use to complain about feeling cold, even while she was getting sunburnt. I put my hand on hers. Her skin is dripping wet.

Ines plunges head-first off the end of the jetty into the water. She dives deep. Under water everything is easy and dangerous at the same time. There are sharks lurking everywhere. The diving mask restricts your field of vision. Every stone morphs into the grey head of a moray eel. I've seen it. The surface of the water breaks. My daughter's wet scalp emerges. She removes the mask from her face. Panda eyes from the mascara that has run, a red mark where the rubber seal of the mask was attached. I ask Judith whether we should hire a diving suit with a weight belt for the girls? She doesn't react. Before, Judith still believed in the fairytale of the Arab lady-charmer, of the hawkers in the bazaar who can't help running a hand over every curve of a woman's body. I wish our roles were still so clear-cut.

My wife lies on her towel, stiff as a corpse. The skin on her stomach is turning red. I stand next to her laid-out head and look at her. Ines is clinging to the end of the jetty. She thinks I can't see her fingertips. But I see everything and take it in, just as I have learnt to take in life. I cling to Judith like an idiot. I think she despises me for it. For the strength of the despair with which I love her, with which I try to tether something that has been dangling free for a long time. Splinters from the damp wooden planks on the jetty work their way into my soles. I can't get them out. They are too fine, practically invisible. I could cry, if it wouldn't make my eyes burn with the dryness. I think about the mindlessness of our movements, Judith's puffy eyes afterwards. I make love like waging a war. I try to make my wife believe in the one true passion. That everything is under control, that everything has its place. Nothing is crazy. Elly is our daughter. We need to stand our ground. Otherwise we'll have nothing left. Even when I'm bored to death by our fumblings, I must admit that afterwards the sand suddenly seems to run through the egg-timer more slowly. It relaxes me, even if only for a short while. But now my expression is stony. I nod to Judith one last time. Ines is still hanging under the jetty. Her eyes peek over the edge.

My whole being trembles and shakes as I tramp up the slope to the granite plateau in my trainers. Fast, faster, fastest. I need to be better. Stronger, smarter, richer. Then finally we'll have security. No more questions, no more uncertainty. I don't talk to my wife. Judith is nervous enough as it is because of the whole business with Elly. The only thing that helps stem the maelstrom of thoughts is underwater hunting. I have to be completely present to kill another living being. It requires utter concentration. I thrust into the depths.

I kick the fins on my feet to counteract the current. All I can hear is the rushing in my ears. My lungs are contracting, they are gasping for air, but I force myself to stay under, just a moment longer. Such amazing calm. I'm already seeing stars, I fire my harpoon, almost blind. The fish gets away at the last second. I surface. Even the air is salty here. The waves lap against the boat. I prepare my harpoon for the next dive. I slide into the water. The lead weights around my hips pull me to the seafloor. I lie in wait behind a rock for a shoal of bream. They turn and twist in the water, glittering silver, as if they were a single being. I wait until they have swum right up close to me, then I fire the spear. It impales a bream. Its blood mingles with the sea water then dissolves. The fish is still alive. I pull it behind me on the harpoon line.

Judith and I sit in front of the fish's backbone, gnawed clean; its sea smell fills the room. The girls are outside in the dark. They are on the rocks on the beach, watching for meteor showers. The damp towels are hanging over the backs of the chairs, the women's bikinis are dripping in the bathroom. Judith's hair must be hard and tangled with the salt drying on it. The speakers on Judith's computer aren't ideal for Chopin. The laptop casing vibrates on the stone kitchen island. I slide a napkin under the computer. The fan hisses, the plastic cover glows. The music patters up the scale. I sidle over to Judith, lay my fingers on her shoulder. She tilts her head back slightly, leans against my stomach. I tense my abdominal muscles, the oblique muscles, the side muscles, my core muscles, as if I were putting on a tight pair of trousers. Judith has closed her eyes. That's the signal. My hands touch, knead, rub. I try to work myself up to lust. Judith undoes my flies and I can't stop her feeling for the snail inside. She tickles it, but the snail stays in its shell. Judith sighs. She tries to wave her disappointment away, but eventually she grabs my arse. I feel dizzy. I've probably not drunk enough during the day. I take a swig of red wine in my mouth, suck it through the gaps between my teeth, then I press my lips to Judith's. As she opens her mouth, the red wine flows in. But she doesn't swallow. She coughs. Red droplets spray across the floor. I give up. Then she shuts the door, jams the back of a chair under the handle, and turns up the volume on the computer. By the time the Queen of the Night hits top F, Judith is lying on the tiles underneath me. My knees are sore, rubbed raw. Judith digs her fingers into my back. The sweat runs down my nose, drips onto her face. The very instant everything is over, we are already rolling in opposite directions. Judith feels for the kitchen roll. She wipes herself. My kneecaps and the weals on my back are burning. But then Judith rests her head on my chest and I hold her in my arms. The handle is pushed down from outside. No one says anything. For a while we just listen to ourselves breathing, staring at the smudges of squashed mosquitoes on the white plastered wall. The flytrap on the ceiling is a long spiral-shaped sticky strip.

Do you want a glass of water? Judith stands up and pours one for me, then another for herself. I ask whether we should perhaps think about opening the door again? Our daughters are still locked out after all. Judith shrugs her shoulders. The water from the canister tastes chalky. It makes my teeth go rough. Maybe I'm just imagining it. Judith seems to like the taste. She empties her glass in one go. I'm still lying on the tiles which are pressing against my backbone, making it stiff. Tomorrow I'll do some bends in my exercises. I wish I were in bed already. My stomach separates and spreads softly. I want to detach myself from the stone, but I'm too heavy. The shutter on the window rattles as it swings open. Elly clambers into the room through it. Her eyes flit over my naked body. With my back to her I swiftly pull my trousers up. The zip catches a few pubic hairs. As I sit down I pluck them out. It stings. Judith is wearing a long t-shirt again. She smiles at our daughter. But Elly juts her jaw forward, narrows her eyes. She stomps from one side of the room to the other and slams the bedroom door behind her. The frying pan which was leaning against the tap clatters into the wash basin. Judith's pupils are large and black. I press a finger to my cheek. It's throbbing and pounding inside. I'll have to get the tooth pulled when we get back home. Ines has now opened the door from outside. We sit down at the table again. Judith, Ines, and I chat and butter our bread; Elly joins us. Her knife slips off the table. It falls to the floor, jangling. Judith and I almost bump heads as we bend down to pick it up at the same time. Elly doesn't laugh. She is sitting straight upright. I look her right in the face as I ask: What now?

My child being back again throws me out of kilter. I try to keep away from the pills. After all, there's no reason to be unhappy any more. But I have been playing host to my worries and fears for too long. I can't throw them out that easily. They keep knocking at the door again. I gradually reduce the doses anyway. I taper down. Then everything starts to close in on me again. My hackles are raised. I decide not to let it get me down. I want to be there for my children. I don't want Elly to have a mother who is stoned. So I try to cope without the pills. But just when I'm lulled into a sense of security, when I think I'm free, the films start. They flicker in front of my mind's eye. I can't stop them. While I'm baking a cake, brushing my teeth, ironing my dress. Over and over again I watch my own demise. I see my body sailing off a bridge or hanging limply in the seatbelt in the fog of exhaust fumes. Sometimes I jump in front of a train. I feel the pain. And yet I know that I can't actually kill myself. I don't have the courage. Longing for death is just an outlet for the stress. But it's the one thing that I can't get under control. I pinch myself, I clamp my teeth together, I do press-ups to distract myself. I don't want to go back to the cotton wool of the pills. But my nerves are stretched tight enough to snap. My veins throb in my neck. I tell myself that nothing and no one can make these films come true. But I can't even read to the end of the headlines in the newspapers. Even before the end of the word I can hear pounding: over. End. Gone. These three words are my constant background noise; it stifles all other perceptions. Just as I think I'm going to explode, the death films stop. Gingerly, I raise my head above the parapet. No stones come hurling down onto my skull. I apply some blusher. The brush caresses my skin. I barely have a chance to enjoy the touch before I have to screw my eyes shut again. The sharp edge of a piece of paper slices through my pupil. It comes at me over and over. Slashes my cornea. Slowly, extravagantly. I run round the block. Scoop water into my face. That makes the paper disappear. But as soon as I'm calm, as soon as I try to sit still, the paper cuts into my eye again. It scythes through the jelly-like substance in my eyeball. I go back to my sweet pink friends. Swallow them before I go to sleep. They look so harmless. But they knock me out in thirty minutes or less. I dissolve. Sleep like a stone. I never wake with a start, I never lie awake thinking things over when my sweet pink friends have come to visit. They relax me. In the morning, my head is still fuzzy. I stumble into the bathroom. I can put up with the dizziness, water retention, and weight gain. The tablets wrap an apron of fat round me. My joints swell up. But the pills also lift the ceiling over my head a few centimetres higher. I can stretch and yawn again, I stop picking fights. The mental image of the sharp paper edge milling into my eyeball disappears. It's such a relief. I can't tell anyone about the films, or the sheet of paper. I'm ashamed of this nonsense. At the same time it makes me afraid. I wonder whether the despair will get the better of me some time. I need to make sure it doesn't, at all costs. My children need me. I have to be there for them. I just need a little bit of poison. The doctor says: If only you knew how many people take pills. Don't be so hard on yourself, she says. Do you need one hundred or two hundred? I try to take myself seriously even as a junkie. I look after myself. I look after my children. I'm not mad. But that's what Elly's therapist claims on the phone. She doesn't say it out loud. But she repeats her words slowly and emphatically. As if I'm a foreigner.

The therapist believes that Elly is not my child. That she is a stranger. I'm her mother, I say. I drive off. I need Elly. I can't go back into the darkness. I can't lose her again. It's a matter of life and death.

My name is Rena. Jana. Jasmin. Call me. I'll listen. I was Sunday's child, arriving into the world just in time for dinner. I didn't look at the clock, but I know. I was there after all. My mother was too young. At the weekend she used to spin underneath the disco ball. She would lock the apartment door behind her. I was still too small to open it. When my mother bent over me in the light of dawn I could smell her sweat, the stale smoke in her hair, and the sharp tang coming from her throat. I reached my arms out to her. She pressed her bosom to my face. But on one of these mornings she didn't find me in my bed. The sheet was cold. My mother called for me. She leaned out the window to see if I had fallen out. She looked everywhere for me. But I wasn't in the apartment. I had been screaming. The neighbours rang the doorbell like mad. No one answered. They called the police. They took me to my grandparents' house. From then on I stayed there. My mother never got me back. My grandfather despised me, even if he did show me how to tie up the berry canes or how to hammer a nail straight into a wall. My skin was just a touch darker than his — that was enough. The scars on my back tell the story. I can prove it. It's all true.

In school no one sat next to me. No one ever invited me to their birthday party. The children thought I was odd. The way I looked, the way I talked, the way I behaved. I was living with old people, my grandparents. I knew the big band music from the Musikantenstadl show by heart instead of chart hits. My clothes came from the charity collection box. I was uncool, a loser. I tried make myself fit in. I swotted up on the names of the right singers, I practised a tinkly laugh and told myself jokes in the mirror until the punchline sat right. But still the other kids at school didn't laugh. They thought I was a bit slippery. They were right. No one could hold me. I even slipped through the fingers of the teacher who liked me and let me help out in the school library. I lost myself in the books. But the stories in them were no use. When I snapped the book covers shut, they were gone.

One day I was playing alone in the garden. The neighbour was just raking his leaves. He looked around, then walked over to the fence. He opened his flies and showed me the trunk in his trousers. I don't remember much more. I told my grandparents what happened. They heard what I said. But they didn't react or do anything about it. They turned away and quickly started to talk about something else. I'm not sure how horrible the experience with the neighbour was for me at the time — what the man actually did, whether I didn't actually feel curiosity and arousal alongside fear. I can't remember that moment at the garden fence properly any more. But I know exactly what my grandparents did. They muted me. They acted as if I hadn't said anything. What I wanted was for my grandparents to stop the neighbour from what he was doing, to protect me. Or at least to believe me. But my words fell down a deep, empty shaft. There wasn't even an echo. It didn't matter in the slightest what I said or did. It was as if I was already dead. I didn't exist at all. Eventually I recognised it as an opportunity.

I told the children in school that my father was a British secret agent. That's why he was never around. I told them about my holidays in the Caribbean, the bruises I got from water skiing, slurping lemonade from half a coconut shell. My classmates were amazed. I knew I was fibbing, but it felt real. I began to take what I wanted. I stole. Tiny, useless things, sometimes electronic stuff. Mostly I threw the thing away imme-diately after taking it. Owning things isn't important to me. I just want to belong. Sometimes, I was caught in the act. I would invent a sad story for the department store security or the shop owner. Sometimes I had leu-kaemia, sometimes my mother was on her death bed. My persecutors were thrown into great consternation every time, but their anger when they discovered the truth was even greater.

When I turned twelve, my grandparents gave me up. They told children's services that they were unable to cope. That was true. They weren't making it up. I ended up in a residential school. I ran away from there too. I hitchhiked until I got to the capital city. But I was too timid and squeamish for a life on the streets. I was hungry, I wanted shelter. So I turned to a policeman and said I was a thirteen-year-old British girl who had run away from home. He took pity on me, looked after me. Back at the police station, however, he discovered that I barely spoke English. My ruse was blown. I was sent back to the residential school. But all the same I had worked out where my chances lay.

I invent myself, I play at being me, something new every day. I tell stories to stay alive. I kill off anything that gets in the way. I listen to people's hearts and then I tell them what they want to hear. I lull them in. I use what I see and feel to do it. I take what I have and I bend it. I simply shift the perspective, illuminate the scene from a different angle. Make it brighter. Darker. Overcast. According to preference. Other people deceive to acquire money, power, or other advantages. That's not what it's about for me. I'm just looking for a role to fill, something long term. I've been running for so long. I move from country to country, children's home to children's home. I'm looking for somewhere to call home. Every time I'm picked up, I present as mute or ill. The adults who find me take care of me. I become whatever they desire. A poor child in need of protection. It feels good to be cared for. I gladly play helpless, full of misery. I only hint at the causes. An uncle who abused me. A car accident in which my parents and my brother died. I was the only one who survived, badly traumatised, in a coma to begin with. The couple who find me on the street are shocked. They give me food to eat and a roof over my head. I end up in a children's home. I like it there. I go to school, I get good marks, I make friends with the other children. But one day someone sees me as I'm binding my breasts. The head teacher calls me in for a chat. I admit everything and move on. That's how I do it every time. I have found sanctuary for a few weeks, sometimes months. But at some point my cover is blown. The carers, teachers, and psychologists are appalled. But they can't punish me while I'm still not an adult. They want to cure me, but they can't catch me. I can sense when someone is sowing suspicion. Then I leg it. While I'm on the run I think up the next poor girl. I'm the perfect actress. The newspapers have already reported my death. All I had to do was call one editorial office. The others reprinted it. I imagine my family waiting in vain for the coffin.

Every time I'm uncovered it gets harder to build a new illusion. More and more people are becoming aware. Despite that, I still agree to interviews. I can't resist the temptation. Being important. Real. True. Unmediated. I'm a legend. The team on one talk show are so touched by me that they offer me a job afterwards. The production manager wangles me into the audience telephone lines. I master the job with panache from the very first day. I am good at listening. The viewers complain, rant and rage. I understand them all. I promise them that their wishes will be fulfilled. That the editors regret their omissions. Both sides are happy. The broadcaster because I get rid of the moaners, and the disappointed viewers because I understand them. I'm the only one who is discontented. As soon as I put down the receiver, I have to be myself again. I can't keep that up for long.

I rent a small room in a hostel near the station. One

evening I open the door. I stare at the unmade bed, the clothes horse with my clothes on top and the newspaper covered in my scribbled signature. It smells of the overripe melon which is rotting away on the window sill. The room feels narrow to me, like a carton. Quietly, as if I might disturb someone, I turn round. I leave the room door open. My damp clothes, a few magazines, a torch; the few things I possess, I leave behind. I jump on the next train. Electricity pylons, deserted houses with gabled roofs and carefully tended front gardens, wooden crucifixes, belching factory chimneys, and bundles of waste paper on goods stations flash past the window. I look out, but I don't see the landscape, towns, my fellow passengers. I'm searching inside myself for something I can use, for some props I can repurpose for a new life. I practise on the guests in the onboard restaurant, test out their reaction. I resist the temptation to sensationalise. I adapt my story to a small-screen format. I disguise myself with a Mickey Mouse sweater and shave my eyebrows off. That gives my eyes the air of a rabbit, panicked, staring. I nick my face with the razorblade too. By the time I get off, I'm someone else. The adventure begins.

I curl up on the final stop on a bus route. The driver finds me. But he's suspicious. Panic rises in me briefly. I'm now well over eighteen, the age of criminal responsibility. I know I'm putting my liberty on the line. The police say I'm committing fraud. Supposedly I'm obtaining benefits by deception. If the bus driver doesn't buy that I'm a child, I'll definitely be sent down this time. I don't let him touch me. I shield my bloody face with my hands. I babble incomprehensibly, lash out. He takes me to a hospital, then to supported housing. There they take me for a traumatised teen. The support workers accept the fact that I don't give them a name, address, family members. I claim to have lost my memory. I am wearing clothes with no labels in, nothing about me gives an obvious indication of where I'm from. One young female doctor is particularly solicitous in her care. She tolerates my snarling and silence. Every day she moves her chair a little bit closer to me. She is pleased that I seem to be starting to trust her. I slowly thaw. For a while I live scot-free. One day a court has to decide who or what will bear the costs of my housing. It's a purely formal process. When I appear before the court, the judge responsible looks me up and down. She leafs through my files. My carer asks: How long will it last? She has another appointment. The judge doesn't look up. It will take as long as it takes, she says. She looks me right in the face. She asks my name, my place of birth. I shrug my shoulders. My memory loss is already on record. The judge furrows her brow. She continues, according to my files I'm a minor. My carer nods. The judge says I don't look underage though. She requests a test. And she wants to add my fingerprints to the database. I blink. That mustn't happen. Because then she would not only find out that I'm an adult, but also about the arrest warrant.

The telephone in my carer's office is my only chance. I call various children's aid organisations. I claim to be a police superintendent and sitting next to me is a young female teenager with memory loss, who must surely have been reported missing. I describe my own appearance. I remain vague in the details, so that as many people as possible come into consideration. Finally I strike lucky. A woman remembers Elly disappearing without trace. The girl is a lot younger than me, but I think I can make it work. I ask the woman for a photo. The fax is black and white and blurred. I cheer when I see it. Elly is still a child. She doesn't have any remarkable features. No unusually knobbly nose, no squint teeth. I think I can make out some similarity with my own features. Elly is the first role that I don't dream up. Elly comes to me. She is a puppet. I borrow her. I tell the judge who I am. I'm Elly. I feel free. I wipe away my own misgivings. But then I download a higher resolution image of Elly. When I see it, my stomach flips over: Elly's eyes are much lighter than mine. Even at the age of eleven, four years ago, she was almost as tall as I am now. How can I pretend to have hardly grown? I'll do what I can. I delete the photo. I dye my hair. I put in blue contact lenses. But I'm sure it's not enough.

Shortly afterwards, the carer knocks at my door. Elly's parents have travelled here. They are waiting in the visiting room. I'm afraid to stand before them. They will see immediately that I'm not their lost daughter. Then they will hit me, curse me, and punish me. I bite my lips nervously. I'm at a loss. If I tell the truth, I'll have to go to prison immediately. But when I look Elly's parents in the eyes, they'll probably have me arrested as well. There's just a tiny chance that I can survive that first moment at least, that I can fool them in the short term. I don't have any choice. The carer is knocking for the third time already.

I pull the hood of my sweater deep over my face and put on sunglasses. I shrink into my clothes. This way I look delicate and fragile. I move slowly, carefully. Elly's parents need to see how scared I am. I am actually afraid right now, I'm all too vulnerable. I stumble into the room. Elly's parents believe that my aversion stems from my experiences over the last four years. I have never mentioned abuse up till that point. It's the people who take me in who put two and two together about my behaviour in this way. I'm happy to be taken for a damaged child, even though I'm twenty years old. Children are allowed to play whenever they want.

Elly's mother's voice trembles as she speaks to me. Her eyes are swimming. Elly's father sniffs. I'm ready to run away when they embrace me. They confirm to the judge that I am their child. Before the official hearing they show me photos of my sister, the house, my friends and relatives. As if they want to drum into me what I need to get my bearings in my new life. They blame my slips on trauma. Thanks to the parental coaching with the photo album, I'm not caught out by the judge's questions. The judge puts her stamp on my new identity. Even the border guards don't cause any difficulties. I am travelling on Elly's child ID card. Only Elly's sister remains reticent. She never looks me in the eyes. Once, when we're alone, she holds out a hand to me and wishes me lots of luck. So I'm sure she knows. But she doesn't do anything about it. I've given myself the gift of a new life. Elly's life. Finally, I've arrived; I'm home, finally. From videos and photos, I learn to swing on my chair like Elly. I repeat the old stories that Ines tells me to Elly's parents and vice versa. Everyone gets excited by my memories returning.

I'm still uneasy all the same. I'm not used to living with other people. Elly's parents and sister are watching me the whole day long. I'm not allowed to be alone.

There's always one of them with me. Do you have everything you need? Do you want something to eat? Something to drink? Are you cold? Do you want to play cards? Should we shut the window? It takes a lot of effort to stay calm. I disguise my voice, I'm practically whispering. I never bathe in front of them. I never forget to wear my contact lenses and hide the solution behind the panels in the bathroom. I mustn't forget myself. I am Elly. Everything is part of that. Even a sniff or a yawn could give me away.

But with every new day a little bit of my fear dissipates. I'm stronger than Elly. I suppress my memory. What I am is becoming reality. Elly's parents feed me. I'm a cuckoo in the nest. But I still don't feel secure. I wonder what happened to the real Elly. I don't believe that her parents genuinely love me. I no longer believe they are taken in by my deception. There must be another reason that they are keeping me in the family. Do they need me for an alibi? Did they bump their Elly off? Or do they know who did it? The thought unsettles me. Every night I awake with a start from my sleep and expect to see an axe above me in the moonlight. But Elly's parents don't kill me. I secretly dig around in the garden. I don't find anything. Elly's father notices the freshly turned earth. He pats it down again. My temples are practically exploding, even though I'm crouching quietly in front of the television. The newsreader dissolves into flickering dots. Elly's father holds out a hand to me and pulls me up. He leads me over to the sofa. He wants us to sit down together. His arm around my shoulders is heavy like a bar.

In secret I call my real mother and tell her that I have new parents. Once she understands that I have completely transformed myself now, that her daughter no longer exists, she hangs up. She doesn't want to have anything to do with me any more. But I have a new home now. I'm lonelier than ever before, always on my guard. I compartmentalise myself, I become sullen, angry. Inside, I'm practically bursting. Elly's parents and her sister believe my bad mood is their fault. They fawn on me. They never leave me in peace. I am standing in front of the mirror in the bathroom. Ines knocks at the door. She throws my towel at my feet. It is full of blood. That's what I dream. Every night. By day I'm dull and monosyllabic through tiredness. I make mistakes, I forget the contact lenses. No one says anything. We are living in a heavy bell jar. Elly is my demon. She is nesting inside me. I can't cast her out. I am Elly. I don't have another role yet.

My unease is growing. The tension is practically tearing me apart. I need to talk to someone. That's why I request that the police officers interview me one more time. The policewoman has been asking for ages. I am supposed to help her catch the perpetrators. No other girl should suffer like I did. Her sympathy moves me. I want to give her what she desires. I tell her in full detail how I was abused and tortured, passed from hand to hand. Her eyelashes flutter. Her voice sounds strained. She thanks me several times for my courage. At the end she embraces me firmly. Now I need to go to identity parades. On the transparent side of the one-way mirror I shake my head. The policewoman is disappointed. She drives me home.

The next day a new female doctor asks me the same questions several times in a row. I start to have doubts, get muddled, don't finish my sentences. The doctor looks me up and down and writes something in her notebook. I am not satisfied with my performance. Elly's parents pick me up. I would love to scream at them and ask what they have done with Elly. I'm sure they know what happened to her. She had a raging fever, went into convulsions, and her father passed her the wrong medication. Or she fell through the balcony railings that her mother had been meaning to repair for ages. Or maybe there's a second family on the other side of the Taunus mountains. Another wife, two delightful daughters. Who don't know about Elly and Ines, or Judith. Who complain about how frequently Hamid is away, his forgetfulness, his workaholism. Who are pleased when he shows up and brings presents for them that he can't actually afford. A man who wants to do right by everybody, and is working himself into the ground between the two fronts that he himself opened up and has kept secret. He spends one evening with Judith, the next in the other house. He mixes up the names, birthdays, friends, and needs. Elly discovers his double life. Her father panics at the thought of the avalanche that will engulf him. Instead of confessing to the mothers, he holds the cushion over this daughter's face and waits until she stops twitching. He disposes of the corpse in hydrochloric acid in the shed, dissolves it. Hamid is still, deep water. Judith is supremely organised, but underneath complete chaos reigns. She breaks out in sweat if a flavour of yoghurt is sold out. Seems entirely plausible that she might lose her hard-won composure in one of these moments of everyday catastrophe. To have peace and quiet at last. I'm sure that they are both in on the secret, and now I'm their bargaining chip, the living proof of their innocence. Judith and Hamid know I have to keep silent if I want to carry on being Elly. I don't have any choice. The wind whistles round the corners of the clinic. Judith, Hamid, Ines, and I walk across the almost empty car park. We get into the car. Silently we slip through the night. The hairs on my arm are standing on end now. Hamid starts to talk to himself. He is dreaming of holidays. Ines's gaze is boring into my side. Her mother turns to me. She asks: Elly? Are you still awake?

Our suitcases are standing in the hallway. We haven't unpacked them yet. Outside the window, the trains rattle past, aeroplanes thunder, cats fight. But we are slumbering. We are not dreaming. My parents are asleep even when they are awake. They sleepwalk through day and night. I'm slowly getting used to it. I'm not allowed to wake them. Only Elly sleeps deeply. Her eyelids are open just a crack. I can see the white of her eyes. I stand by her bed for a long time. She doesn't stir. Later, the rain stops. It's just drizzling now. Elly takes her new bike out of the garage. I stand in her way. I ask her: Where did we hide the horseshoe that time? I'm talking about the rusty iron that I won ten years ago in the sack race. That should be enough of a clue. But Elly isn't concerned about passing my test. What do you take me for, she says, and grins at me. Her mouth puckers, wide and provocative. The black gap of her missing top tooth sucks me in. I am in danger of losing myself in it. But Elly wheels the bike out to the field. The countryside is as flat as a plate. Out here there are hardly any trees, no buildings. I can see Elly far away across the fields. I follow her in secret. I want to see what she gets up to. She cycles around aimlessly. I hide behind a haystack. Elly cycles with no hands for long stretches. Her arms dangle next to the saddle. She whistles to herself. Sometimes she closes her eyes, as if to test whether anything will happen to her. Nothing does. Elly doesn't fall. She is careful. She reaches for the handlebars on the uneven gaps between the paving slabs. She swerves puddles. She doesn't want to get dirty. She waves to a few horses. Whistles with two fingers when the animals don't respond. She dismounts once. She picks some poppies, although the flowers' red petals flutter away from her as she cycles. Out there, on her own, she seems carefree. All her hesitancy has disappeared. She pedals resolutely. The spokes of the wheels whirl, tracing spirals. Elly flies over the path on her bike. The sky is high and piercingly blue. Not a cloud. Crows and starlings hop over the stubble in the fields. It smells of burnt Plexiglas. There was an accident in the nearby factory. A rabbit runs across the furrows. My eyes follow it for a moment. My heart is beating evenly, my breath is controlled. In and out. I am mindful of breathing out for longer than I breathe in. When I was in hospital I practised letting go for hours at a time. I relaxed one muscle after the other, until I was a human blancmange. I can still do it perfectly to this day. From my feet to the top of my head. First tense, and then let go. I hesitate before I turn back to Elly. When Elly came back, my parents and I thought we had put the worst behind us. Today I know that torture is a notion that can keep on multiplying infinitely. A jay chatters in the trees behind me. The leaves don't rustle. The clouds, the grass, even the birds in the sky seem to be frozen. I hesitate before I turn back to Elly. When I finally do, she's just a tiny speck. Her silhouette melts into the trees in the wood. Then she is gone.

This story is my story. I'm the one who is missing from it. This story isn't lying there in the street, it isn't sleeping in our house any more, and nothing and no one is one step ahead of me. I'm not stuck in a cage, I'm not a prostitute. I have never put on a disguise. My story begins at a crossroads on a red bike.

A siren screams. The cars brake and clear a path. An ambulance drives across the crossroads, missing my sports bag by a hair's breadth. It has slipped off my pannier rack. The red bike topples onto the kerb. I drop it. The wheels spin in the air. I run to the middle of the road. The asphalt softens under my feet. I start to sink, to wade. The tar sticks to my ankles, viscous and gluey. I want to take my shoes off and run. But I don't make it. The sports bag with my judo suit in is lying on the markings in the middle of the road. I got the green belt last week. The suit mustn't get dirty. The cars only brake for a moment. The lights will turn green any second. The headlights are shining on me. The motors screech. The cars set off and I feel a hard blow. Then nothing. Nothing I can feel. Nothing that I want. Darkness.

I sleep and wake and wake and sleep. Nothing ever stops. I slide down the glowing rays of the rising sun into a cave. Water is flowing down the sides of the walls, it streams into the middle of the tunnel, joins together to form a river. First it splashes, then it gurgles, and behind a rock the water tumbles into a broad stream. It foams and swirls, plunges over a cliff. The rushing noise fills me entirely. I fly, light as air. I stream into the cave. I am a wave in the water, I swim without getting wet. I bubble like the water, sparkling inside. I see but I have no eyes. I feel but I have no skin. Suddenly everything is bright, dazzling. I put my hands over my face. The lid of a car boot is floating above me. Someone drags me out into the open. Pushes me onto the damp leaves. I can smell the rain. The car door thunders. The tyres spin in the mire. The tracks are clearly visible. But I'm lying in the mud, I don't move.

Later, I stagger to my feet. My stomach is growling. My legs are trembling. The bushes and trees around me have shapeshifted into giant black caterpillars. The furry monsters crawl towards me. I quickly limp towards the road. The darkness here is less frightening. There is a path. It leads me out of here. I walk and hiss at myself: Keep going. Don't give up. Doesn't matter which direction. Am I injured? I don't want to know. I don't feel for injuries. The dampness on my cheeks must be rain. Blood would be warm. I must keep going. I urge myself onwards. I mustn't turn round or panic. I carry on walking. I never arrive.